TOXIN

TERROR IN THE HEARTLAND

6666

GEORGE WHITE

Wasteland Press

www.wastelandpress.net
Shelbyville, KY USA

Toxin 666:
Terror in the Heartland
by George White

First Printing – November 2016
ISBN: 978-1-68111-146-9
Library of Congress Control Number: 2016956669

Printed in the U.S.A.

0   1   2   3   4   5

AUTHOR'S NOTE

This post 9/11 story is pure fiction. I've taken the liberty of creating fictitious characters whose lives intersect in Iowa in September 2001. It is an imaginary tale woven into history, set in beautiful West Branch and vital Iowa City, Iowa. (West Branch has its own small-town vitality and Iowa City its own brand of Big Ten beauty.) Thanks to those two communities for permitting my characters to visit them.

I also want to thank my brother Dale White, for the initial inspiration for the tale. My brother Myron White, cousin Ron Sleeter, son-in-law Travis Blair, nephew Stephen White and niece Kali VanBalle gave me invaluable input. Others who helped me included Steve Sands, Detective Phil Yerington, Dr. Ezra Sidran, Victoria Henning, Shari Cole, Jeanne Wolf, Betty Nezerka and Lynn Calvert. Iowa City Library and West Branch High School provided valuable resources.

A special thanks to my wife Martha, for her encouragement.

CHAPTER ONE:
Dead Wrong

Tuesday, September 4, 2001

University of Iowa Professor John Egstrom always stuck to his routine. A Few students liked his predictability; most considered him a pompous neurotic. As usual, he sat alone at his breakfast table in the Memorial Union, a glass of milk near his left hand and a bagel with cream cheese and grape jelly in his right. The cafeteria workers knew better than to run out of grape jelly. It had happened only once. Egstrom was taking the first bite into his bagel when someone hit him from behind and almost knocked over his glass of milk. He whirled and was assaulted by a clumsy apology.

Egstrom interrupted, "Don't I know you?"

His assailant mumbled, "Yes. I was in your advanced bio chem. class."

The irate teacher said. "I remember you, you clumsy oaf. All that UCLA hype about you was bogus. You disappointed me. You still disappoint me. Get out of my sight!"

The rebuked student scurried away to a table on the far side the room, along the windows. Egstrom shook his head and went back to eating his breakfast. Irritated, he hurriedly took bites of bagel and gulps of milk. When finished, he tried to look at his papers, but his eyes wouldn't focus. His face contorted as he vomited and sprawled across the table, his body twitching uncontrollably.

Students and café workers watched in shock and horror; but the one sitting by the windows smiled. He enjoyed watching the professor flop on the floor, like a freshly-landed fish. No one saw the slight scruffy figure slip out of the room as the paramedics rushed in. People never noticed him unless he was in the classroom or the laboratory. There he was a star, top of his class. "Dr. Egstrom, you were wrong about me! Dead wrong."

CHAPTER TWO:
Start-Over

Tuesday, September 4, 2001

"Dad! Where is it?" Paul Lovejoy hollered up from the kitchen. He mumbled to himself, "I can't even find the toaster, how am I ever going to find my way around a new school? Good thing we got to Iowa on Saturday." They had unpacked his school clothes yesterday, but had not found all the kitchen stuff. Surrounded by half-opened moving boxes, Paul didn't know where to look. "Dad, I need some help down here!"

The old floorboards creaked above the kitchen. Paul hoped his dad wouldn't fall through. You could hear everything in this old wreck of a house. He was a senior in high school and had not wanted to move to Iowa in the first place. All his friends were back in Illinois. 'Why do we have to live in this ramshackle house out in the country? Why couldn't we find a better place?' Before the accident, Paul had lived to play football. But those days were over. The West Branch football team had started practice a month ago and it was too late to make the squad. His dad had telephoned the coach last week. The coach described his successful football program, but was not encouraging, "Sorry Mr. Lovejoy, we're pretty strong in all

3

positions." Hearing this, Paul decided not to even try out. He didn't want to spend his senior year standing on the sidelines. It was his Dad's fault.

"Dad, are you coming down or what?"

His father shuffled down the narrow staircase, rubbing his eyes and trying to button his flannel shirt.

"Dad, you've buttoned your shirt crooked. You going to work disguised as a lumberjack?"

"Put a lid on it kid! My shift doesn't start until 3:00 pm." Re-buttoning his shirt, he added, "By the way, you're becoming a real pain in the...."

"Watch your language Mr. LoveJOY. I'm still a malleable minor." Paul saw no hint of a smile on his father's face, but continued, "Anyway, it isn't much fun being around you anymore. You wander around like a zombie on sleeping pills. You don't whistle your annoying tunes anymore. I wish you'd live up to the family name the way you used to." On a roll, he chided, "You don't even watch football anymore!"

"Paul, I still like football. In fact, I hope to get us tickets to Saturday's Iowa game. I know it's not our beloved Illinois, but it's still the Big Ten. Consider it an early birthday present!"

"Do you even know who the Hawkeyes are playing?"

"I might dress like a lumberjack and act like a zombie, but I'm still very much alive! Iowa plays Miami of Ohio on Saturday. In Iowa's opener, last week, they beat Kent State 51 to zip!"

"I heard the Kent State game when we drove out here," Paul said. "I'm trying to get used to being in Iowa and not Illinois. What did you think of Iowa's game?"

"Sorry, I was too busy driving the U-Haul to pay attention."

"Dad, I offered to drive the truck," Paul's voice softened. "I know interstate driving isn't easy for you. I get it. You can make it up to me on Saturday by taking me to the game. We never got to see the Illini play."

"We watched them on TV."

4

"That's not the same as being there. Get us tickets. You can hit up one of your new University friends. You already know people here. They want you."

Herb got the message. "Paul, you'll make friends at school. Today's just your first day of classes. Let's plan on the Iowa game Saturday."

"The game's OK, but there are no friends here, just a bunch of strangers. I don't want to be here! There's the bus, I gotta' go. Forget the toaster and the toast." Grabbing his backpack, he opened the door.

Lovejoy half-shouted, "Strangers are just friends waiting to happen!" After watching his son run to the bus, he walked across the kitchen and kicked the pile of boxes next to the table. When the top two bounced to the floor, the missing toaster smiled up at him from a grocery store banana carton. Too late! Paul was already getting on the bus. 'It's not his fault. I forced him to come out here. He's a good kid.' Herb sighed, walked over to the counter and carefully picked up the CD. He could still see her smudged fingerprints on the case. He played it again, as he'd done every day since he was released from the hospital two years ago. Herb Lovejoy leaned against the counter, drank his coffee and listened to Whitney Houston's bitter-sweet words, "I will always love you."

CHAPTER THREE:
Anxious

Tuesday, September 4, 2001

Jerry Kerr poured a fresh cup of coffee for his wife Marilyn. He listened to WHO radio's farm report while she fixed breakfast. When she joined him at the table, he switched to KHAK, a country music station. The couple were old rock-and-rollers whose music tastes were shifting toward country. Breakfast conversations centered on the farm and her work as a high school guidance counselor. "Sick cows and sick kids, that's all we talk about," he once said. She wanted to disagree but felt the bite of truth in his words. Today's breakfast talk centered on the upcoming dairy tour they were hosting on Thursday.

Jerry lamented, "I don't know how we'll ever get everything ready. I'm running out of feed, and it's rained so much I can't get out in the field to chop corn. The hired man is off, a feed salesman is coming today, and I've still got a sick cow." Jerry's cows were his business but he often got too attached to them.

"Did you hear that?" she asked.

"Hear what?" he said.

"Turn up the radio. I love this song by Diamond Rio."

He turned up the volume and both listened.

"Last night I had a crazy dream. A wish was granted just for me. It could be for anything. I didn't ask for money or a mansion in Malibu. I simply wished for one more day with you."

"We don't just have one more day Jerry, we've got two! Two days to get ready, and we've done this tour gig before," she teased.

"Not when it had rained for forty days and forty nights!" Jerry said.

Marilyn smiled, "You still remember a few things from Sunday School."

He blew her a kiss and said, "Careful with those romantic country songs. I could wish for a thousand more days with you...but I'd really like a few days without rain."

Marilyn replied, "Aren't you the romantic one? Maybe you'd prefer sleeping on the couch for a week?" She waved, grabbed her purse and headed out the door for the six-mile drive to West Branch High. Jerry enjoyed watching her walk away. Even though she shrugged off his comparisons with Marilyn Monroe, it was her figure that first caught Jerry's eye. Now that she was fifty-eight, her figure was fuller, she wore looser clothes and her blonde hair was turning gray like her mother's. But her curves still turned his head.

Jerry told himself to stop day-dreaming. He pulled on his rubber work boots and walked through his own pre-tour farm tour. He surveyed the buildings, hoping she would be right about being ready. Jerry was the third generation of Kerrs to operate this dairy farm. He wished he could feel prouder of how he'd kept the place up. The dilapidated red barn, which was no longer red and no longer housed cattle, desperately needed a coat of paint. His dairy cows had been promoted up the hill to a newer free stall barn he'd built twenty years ago, but even it showed signs of aging. Jerry felt that way about himself.

His boots sucked in the mud as he quickened his pace, "I better check on old number 230 and see if she's had her calf yet." She was his top milk producer from a long family line of winners. "Grandpa would call me a liar if I told him that number 230 produced 33,000 pounds of milk last year. I was surprised myself." Jerry knew a nine-year-old cow was old in cow-years. Old cows, like first-time heifers, often had more trouble calving. Dairy cows needed to kick out a calf every year to maximize production. This could be his prize cow's last calf which thanks to artificial insemination would be sired by one of the best bulls in the country. Jerry had splurged big-time, wanting the genetic dynasty to carry on. He fantasized about setting a new state milk production record before retiring.

That dream bubble popped when Jerry stepped into his three-pen maternity barn. He didn't like what he found. Number 230 was in trouble. The calf's front legs protruded in mid-birth, and the cow seemed to have given up. Jerry tried to help her deliver her calf, but knew he needed the veterinarian. He wiped his hands on his coveralls and rushed to his office telephone. It was not much of an office - just an old table, a telephone, an adding machine with a spool of white tape, stacks of farm records and an assortment of tools in the corner.

Jerry grabbed the phone and called his veterinarian, Doc Jarrett. It was one of five numbers he had on speed dial. After four rings, a recording kicked in, "Sorry, I can't take your call. Leave a message and I'll get back to you as soon as I can." Kerr left an urgent message and rushed back to check on the cow. She was now lying on her side in the maternity stall. The longer it took, the more likely the calf would be still-born. Several times, in situations like this, he'd lost both the cow and the calf. He went back to his office and collapsed into his old beat-up black chair next to the phone.

'Ring…ring…ring.' His phone startled him. He grabbed for it and almost knocked it off the table. "Thanks Doc. See you in a few minutes." There still might be time. Jerry checked the cow and listened for the vet.

He heard something and hurried to the barn door. 'Damn, it's just the school bus!'

CHAPTER FOUR:
Uprooted

Tuesday, September 4, 2001

Kelly Sanders fidgeted at the front window, 'Where is that school bus?' She still had half an hour to wait but was an impatient eighteen-year-old. Kelly wasn't happy about being forced to move from New York City to Iowa for her senior year in high school. She wished her over-educated parents had chosen to teach somewhere else. She was OK with the University of Iowa but Iowa City was so small that the population would fit into a New York City block. Her parent's dream home was her nightmare. It was out in the middle of nowhere, surrounded by cornfields, trees, pastures and cows. Her parents had become sick of their daily commute to Cornell's Weill Center for Medical and Biological Research in Manhattan's Upper East Side. It was a grueling 90-minute trip to the elite school where they taught and did research. The couple gladly traded their New York brownstone for a custom-built log mansion in rural Iowa. Her parents loved it but barely had time to sleep here. Success had a high price.

She walked to the spacious den and found her parents rushing to gather up papers, brief cases and laptops. Their expertise made them a hot commodity in research but they always seemed too busy for time with her. The move to Iowa had made things worse.

Her mother apologized, "Honey, sorry we have to leave early again. It's going to be one of those days - classes, meetings, seminars, and research to oversee…"

Kelly blurted, "You're both always too busy to talk to me. You may be great researchers, but you've not been such great parents to me and Maria."

"Back off, young lady!" Ruth Sanders said as she slammed her briefcase on the desk. "You have no idea what I'm going through." She pointed to overflowing stacks of papers and scientific journals on the side table. "Do a little light reading and you might figure out what we deal with every day!"

Her father intervened, "We've got to go. Kelly, there's a new box of granola in the cupboard and yogurt in the fridge. We'll talk later." He threw her a smile as they rushed to the garage. Her mother didn't look back.

Kelly whirled and stomped back into the living room. She and her mother often rubbed each other the wrong way. The teen gave her dog a big hug, "Darth, Kelly loves you." Even Darth's name was a source of tension. When Kelly was ten she'd named him "Darth." Her mother couldn't believe it. "Well, Mother, why not? My puppy is totally black and will be as good as Darth Vader was bad." She had left her Star Wars phase behind long ago. Today, she was more interested in seeing the school bus. Kelly tousled her best friend's head. Darth licked her hand, as if to say, "I'm here." She knew he would always be there for her. He had saved her life.

CHAPTER FIVE:
Pressured

Tuesday, September 4, 2001

The pager buzzed. Dr. Ruth Sanders knocked over a stack of documents as she reached to answer it. She mumbled, admonishing herself. Sometimes her ability to concentrate was a liability. She was a driven person who commanded respect. No one in the Bio Med Building dared to call her 'Dr. Ruth.' "What is it Linda?"

Her assistant stuttered, "Dr. Egstrom… Dr. Egstrom is gone."

Sanders knew the name. Egstrom was a prominent tenured professor in her department. He was both a researcher and faculty member. "Linda, what do you mean 'gone'?"

"He's gone, passed…dead."

Sanders asked, "When? How?"

Linda said, "This morning. The Iowa City Police just called. They said Egstrom's death was sudden and suspicious. He died in the Memorial Union Cafeteria. They won't say anything official until after the autopsy. We talked some more and the cop blurted out that it looked like a poisoning to him. He didn't think suicide at breakfast was likely, so it's being investigated as a homicide."

Ruth Sander's usually nimble mind froze. After an awkward moment, she said, "This is not good. Linda, we need to check his class schedule. Does he have a family?"

"I don't think I ever met him," Linda apologized in her flat mid-western accent. She had been hired just a week before Sanders came to Iowa City and was still learning the ropes.

"That's OK. Find his class schedule. I'll see if he has family here." Sanders leaned back in her chair, caught her breath and turned to her computer console. She logged into her personnel files and looked up Dr. John Egstrom. He was forty years old and single. The only family listed was a sister in New Jersey. Egstrom had been on the U of I faculty for eight years. His research creds were impressive, but his student evaluations were not. Six complaint letters were in his file from disgruntled students who thought they deserved better grades. But two complaints were more serious. Both accused Egstrom of being "insensitive, rigid and abusive." No official reprimands were listed. Sanders was wondering about that, when Linda interrupted her.

"Dr. Sanders, I have Egstrom's schedule for this week. He has a 1:00 pm lecture today on "Toxicology... and cell research."

Sanders picked up on Linda's confusion. "Toxicology is the science of poisons."

"Poisons!" Linda exclaimed as she made the connection between the lecture topic and the possible cause of death. Both were struck by the irony of a poison professor dying by poisoning.

Sanders brought them back to reality, "We need to follow protocol. Who do we have listed as backup for Egstrom's classes?"

Linda sneezed and apologized. Her hay fever was kicking in. "I'll get on it!" She hurried to her desk, wiped her eyes with the 100th Kleenex of the day and wondered how Dr. Sanders could be both so smart and so together.

Ruth Sanders was trying to hold it together. The death had rattled her.

CHAPTER SIX:
Greenhorn

Tuesday, September 4, 2001

Herb Lovejoy was trying to restart his life. He drove west on Interstate 80 from West Branch toward Iowa City to begin his 3:00-11:00pm hospital shift. Road construction at the Dubuque Street exit slowed traffic to a crawl. He got to University Hospital and found what must have been the last parking spot within a mile. He squeezed his white Corolla into a narrow space next to a blue SUV, jumped out of the car and sprinted to the hospital. His son Paul would not have called it sprinting. "That's OK son. You'll be forty-five someday too!"

He hurried through a construction area and entered the south door. Once inside, the maze of hallways, waiting rooms, clinics and specialty floors was bewildering. Gasping for breath, he tried to remember where he was going. Getting his bearings, he spotted his new boss's office. As he walked in, Elaine Armstrong, veteran Spiritual Care Director of University Hospital, welcomed him. "Reverend Lovejoy, come on in. Please take a seat." She pointed to the padded chair, on the left, in front of her desk. She took the other chair. Armstrong's office walls were crammed with book cases, family pictures and certificates. Herb had been impressed with the competence she demonstrated during the interview process. The director looked to be about sixty, with short salt-and-pepper hair. She was well-dressed but did not seem concerned with high fashion.

After a few pleasantries, she asked, "How was the move from Joliet? Is your son Paul adjusting to the idea of a small-town Iowa school?"

"We got here Saturday. I guess the move was OK, but I don't want to give U-Haul any business for a decade or two. Paul starts school today. I think he's a little nervous."

"How are you doing?" she asked.

Herb gave her his usual expanded version of "fine".

"I'm really asking a deeper question, Herb. Your answer may determine how well you fit in as a chaplain."

He dreaded what else she might say. Clinically trained chaplains, although known for their listening skills, could ask probing personal questions.

"Herb, you've been through a lot of losses, not the least of which is the death of your wife and daughter. You are changing jobs and have moved to a new state. Big changes like these can affect your interactions with patients and families. They can sensitize you to the hurting, or they can weigh you down."

He squirmed, "That's all too true. I'm still struggling to process everything."

She leaned forward, "Herb, that's an honest response. I want to assure you that our Spiritual Care Team will work with you as you sort through this. We're each working through our own stuff."

He thought she seemed to have it all together.

She added, "Remember that God uses wounded healers. We find strength as we struggle and stumble our way along." He hoped she was right.

Armstrong stood, signaling that their meeting was over. Herb stood and knocked over a stack of books on the side table. He apologized, picked them up and tried to restack them. 'What order had they been in?' he wondered. Herb froze when he picked up the last book - a familiar slim paperback. He hadn't touched it in two years, though he'd given it to dozens of grieving families.

Director Armstrong saw his hesitation. "Go ahead. Take it. *Good Grief* is a classic. I have several other copies." She shook his hand warmly and said, "Welcome to our team. Meet me after your Hospital Orientation session and I'll bring you up to speed on departmental procedures."

Herb closed the door and walked down the hall while thumbing through Granger Westberg's book on grieving. He looked at the index and saw the familiar stages of grief listed: shock, depression, physical distress, panic, guilt. Distracted by the book, he almost collided with a nurse in scrubs. Apologizing, he shoved the paperback into his jacket pocket. Herb hurried to his orientation meeting, wondering why he was still stuck on the "guilt" stage of grief.

An hour later Herb returned to Armstrong's office. She put him through the required training drill and took him to his new office on the second floor. She handed Herb two fat ring binders filled with information. "Read through these. You're welcome to eat at your desk, or go to the cafeteria. I'll be back at 6:00pm and introduce you to the chaplain you'll be partnering with today. You're now officially on the Spiritual Care Team, here is your personalized University Hospital ID badge. After he put it on, she handed him a stack of business calling cards. He saw the gold dome of Iowa City's Old Capitol embossed in the upper right hand corner of the cards. She tapped his binders on the way out and smiled, "Happy reading!"

Herb waded through pages and pages of rules and regulations. His eyes burned and he was getting a headache. After a quick meal downstairs, he returned to his desk just as Director Armstrong knocked on his door. "Chaplain Lovejoy I want you to meet Chaplain John Conner." Conner was about Herb's age and wore a clerical collar identifying him as a clergyman. His eyes sparkled with a whimsical blend of humor and cynicism. He sported a well-trimmed goatee and a wedding ring.

"You'll shadow John in the NICU this afternoon. It's both a heart-warming and heart-breaking place. Expect a little bit of both!" she added on her way out. It took Herb a second to remember that NICU stood for Neonatal Intensive Care Unit.

Chaplain Conner said, "Guess we're close enough in size for you to be my shadow."

Patting his own thinning hair, he added, "Looks like we have the same hair stylist, too. When it comes to shadowing, I have two rules - stay close and stay behind me. Watch and learn before you lead."

"Makes sense," Herb answered.

"Before we go, let's sit down and chat for a minute. Chaplains need to work together like soldiers in a foxhole. The hospital is a battleground between life and death. People's emotional lives often depend on us. Enough military images - tell me about yourself. How did you end up here?"

Herb squirmed, "It's a long story...."

"Give me the Reader's Digest version," John said.

"Two years ago, we were in a car accident. My wife and daughter were killed." Herb hesitated, "My faith was shaken and I didn't know how I could go on preaching. The church had too many memories of Brenda and Sarah." His voice broke. "Grieving has been harder than I ever imagined."

"So you left pastoring a church to become a chaplain?" John asked.

"I guess you could put it that way. I needed a way to make a living and I hoped to find myself again..." He'd said more than he intended to and changed the subject, "What about you John?"

The chaplain answered, "I've been here on staff for ten years. I got burned out by churches. I got sick and tired of the hypocrisy of church people. I felt like a hypocrite and decided to make an honest man of myself, so I came here. As an ex-pastor, you can understand that, can't you?"

Herb nodded and wanted to say, "We can love the church warts-and-all because God loves us that way." But he couldn't. Herb wasn't sure anymore.

John stood up, "We better get going. Two months ago my wife and I were blessed with our first grandchild. We're glad she didn't need NICU care. You take a normal term pregnancy and birth for granted until...." Elevator C's door opened. John punched the 4th floor button and they rode up to the Neonatal Intensive Care Unit.

An efficient nurse pointed to a cramped waiting room. "It's good there are two of you. Bill and Terri Griffin need all the help they can get. Their one-pound, fifteen-ounce newborn baby boy is hanging on by a thread and a prayer. They're all alone."

Conner thanked her and led the way. The Griffins were huddled together on a small brown couch. Griffin was trying to comfort his trembling wife, but both were crying. John reached out to them, "Bill and Terri, I'm John Conner, and this is Herb Lovejoy. We're chaplains here at the hospital. Can we sit with you?"

After a mumbled yes, the chaplains pulled up chairs on each side of the couch. Conner was on the husband's side, Herb beside the wife.

"Tell us what's going on," John asked.

"It's our baby boy," said Terri softly. "I was only 27 weeks along. I should have been more careful. He wasn't supposed to come until Thanksgiving. It was way too early for him to be born. What are we going to do? We haven't even painted the nursery or got him a crib. How can we take him home?"

"Honey, it's not your fault," her husband said. "First, the little guy has to make it through tonight...." Bill broke down. Wiping away his tears with his sleeve, he told them, "Little Billy was born Sunday night."

"He's our first," Terri said. "If it was a boy, I wanted to name him after his daddy."

The Griffins then described their frantic midnight drive from Fairfield. "It's usually a 45-minute drive. I somehow got us here in 30 minutes. I still don't know how I did it."

"I don't remember much," Terri added. "These last two days have been a terrible blur. It's all so confusing. I don't get hospital lingo - NICU, CXR, HFV, NIC, PICC, SO2 ... I just can't remember what all the letters mean."

"The doctors and nurses try to explain," Bill said, "but nothing sinks in. They have to save our baby. We don't have to know what they're doing, but they sure as hell better!"

Terri glanced at the empty chairs in the waiting room and said, "Some of the other families with babies here have helped us. They know what we're going through."

"Do you have family nearby?" John asked.

"My folks are driving back here from Texas and should be here later tonight," Bill replied.

Terri said, "My dad's been gone for three years and mom just got off work to fly here from Michigan."

"I imagine you'll be glad to see them," Herb said.

"You have no idea," Terri sobbed. "I'm almost too old to be a first-time mother, but I still need my own mom."

"I just hope they get here in time," her husband lamented.

"Bill, we can't give up. They'll make it and so will our little Billy!"

A nurse stepped into the waiting room, "Mr. and Mrs. Griffin, we have results from your son's last blood tests and his brain scan." She motioned for them to remain seated but they stood up anyway. Terri was wobbly. Herb looked to John for clues about what to do. The nurse interpreted the dreaded tests.

"Oh, no!" Terri cried out.

Conner stepped in and helped Bill keep her from collapsing. Herb watched and prayed. The fragile thread of life was fraying. All they could do was to wait and pray. Now it was up to the medical team and the tiny baby's will-to-live.

CHAPTER SEVEN:
Frayed

Sometime, 1974

A mother on the west coast hated her baby. His coming had forced her into a hurry-up marriage to the mad genius. Her husband was intriguing and the smartest person she'd ever met. But now, she was stuck in a cramped cracker box house with a man who ignored her and a screaming baby who wouldn't let her rest. He just kept crying, crying, crying! Was it colic, childhood insomnia, personality disorder? Crazy crying! She didn't know if she could stand it anymore.

After high school, she had cut all ties with her family and fled to LA where she hooked up with a bad crowd. Her new bright boyfriend rescued her from them but shackled her forever with this child from Hell. She despised the baby and twice got a pillow to smother his screams. But somehow, the fear of the law or a flicker of maternal instinct had stopped her.

The baby wouldn't take his bottle, so she turned to hers. She needed it to dull her pain. She had no doctors, no nurses and no chaplains to help her. Her brainiac husband knew less about babies, and cared even less. He was obsessed with scientific theories and experiments. The next great discovery was always just around the corner. After they married, she learned that he didn't get his master's degree because he hadn't bothered taking final exams. He thought he already knew the answers to everything. He didn't understand what she was going through.

The baby bawled again. She shook his crib. Her screams drowned out Mac Davis singing *Stop and Smell the Roses*. She listened to the song through her sobs, arguing with the singer, "I ain't got no roses to smell, just this stinky baby." She flipped Danny on his back to change another diaper.

Money woes forced her to get a part-time bartending job at *Sammy's Place*. The sign out front said, "Hot Beer/Lousy Food". She started working May 9th, 1974, the day President Richard Nixon resigned. Gas prices had skyrocketed, and she sold her junker car to pay the rent. She walked to work, leaving the brat with his genius father. She preferred the attention of men at the bar to the squalls of a baby. The food at *Sammy's* was as bad as promised, but the drinks flowed and the crowds grew. Soldiers fresh from the Vietnam War were frequent customers. They appreciated her low-cut, tight barmaid outfit and were good tippers.

"I'd have been better off with one of these wounded warriors," she thought. "But who wants a woman with a screaming baby?" She continued working at *Sammy's Place* through the mid- 1980s. It helped her escape from her life at home but enslaved her to world of whisky and bourbon. She had traded one bottle for another.

CHAPTER EIGHT:
Dog Lover

Tuesday, September 4, 2001

Kelly Sanders waited for the school bus and absently patted her dog's dark head. "I wouldn't be alive today, if it weren't for you Darth!" She stepped across the room and affectionately touched the framed newspaper clipping next to her 8th -grade school photo. The article recounted the fateful day she almost drowned. She read it aloud to Darth.

DOG SAVES NEW YORK TEEN

Thirteen-year-old Kelly Sanders was saved from drowning by her four-year-old black Labrador Retriever. The girl fell into the Neversink River near Woodstock, NY. Her dog, named Darth, pulled her to shore. She was transported to Benedictine Hospital in Kingston. Doctors report that she is in good condition and should expect a full recovery. The Sanders family, of New York's Upper East Side, was vacationing in the Catskills. Both parents are researchers at Weill Medical in Manhattan.

Kelly pointed to the newspaper photo of Darth and her sister Marie, "You're the hero Darth!" Patting him again, she conceded, "I guess Dad and Marie helped too."

Kelly remembered nothing about that day. She had awakened in the hospital with bruises, bandages and a headache. Later, Marie told her how it happened, using her big-sister voice, "Kelly, don't you remember? We were in the Catskills, walking along the river. Darth was leading the way, Dad was way behind us. You wouldn't let me enjoy the scenery, but wanted to banter about our names. You complained that I got named after the famous scientist Marie Curie and you got named for Grandma Sanders. You argued that you should have been named after the scientist."

Kelly had supposedly challenged Marie, "I can walk out further on those slippery rocks than you can."

Marie told her, "My jaw dropped when I saw you step across the churning waters and stand on a rock the size of a basketball. You jumped to the next rock and the next until you were far from shore. Then you slipped. I panicked when you went under and the current swept you down river. I just stood there in shock, but Darth jumped in, swam to you and brought you back to shore. I suppose now he's an official 'Kelly Retriever'!"

Kelly hugged Darth. "Marie was right, you're my Kelly Retriever. Kelly loves you. Kelly loves you!" She could count on him. She gave him another squeeze, "No, don't lick my face. You'll ruin my lipstick. There's the bus." Kelly gave him a farewell squeeze, bolted through the front door and jogged down the driveway, her black sweatshirt flapping behind her, 'Are we out in the boondocks or what?' She boarded the bus without brushing off the dog hair. She wore it as a badge of honor, believing that animals deserved respect. She still wanted a *My Dog Saved My Life* bumper sticker on their BMW.

The kids goofing off in the back of the bus were obviously life-long small-town friends, so Kelly sat by herself behind the driver. The driver was what Kelly called 'Iowa-friendly'. She'd already learned the Iowa wave, which was done by casually waving only two fingers while still gripping the steering wheel; that was not how the finger wave was done back in New York City. She felt the familiar starts, stops, and sways of school bus # 7. She was surprised when they pulled off the blacktop onto a bumpy gravel road. She asked the driver, "New shortcut?"

"Not one I'd choose. Transportation director told me to pick up a new kid," he said.

The extra twisting, jolting, bumpy ride ended in front of a decrepit old house. The student bolted out of the front, slamming the door so hard she thought the house might fall down. Kelly got a better look at the new passenger when the bus door opened. He had wavy dark hair and broad shoulders. She threw him a smile. He hesitated before sliding into the seat beside her.

"Hi, you a West Branch native?" she asked.

"No, just moved here Saturday."

"I moved here in June. My name's Kelly Sanders."

"I'm Paul."

"No last name?"

He missed a beat before answering, "Lovejoy." Then he said, "You don't talk like a Midwesterner."

"You think I have an accent?" Kelly responded. "I'm proud to say I am from New Yawk, as in the Big Apple. We've been here three months, and my mom is still unpacking boxes."

"Wish I had a mom to help us unpack," he said.

"Your folks divorced?"

"No, just no mom! She's gone. Dad's all I've got and I blew up at him this morning."

Kelly sensed that there was an unspoken back story. She was intrigued and drawn to him. 'Maybe this day won't be so bad, after all,' she thought.

CHAPTER NINE:
Long Day

Tuesday, September 4, 2001

Exhausted and hungry, Chaplain Herb Lovejoy left the hospital at midnight. He drove to *The Campus Joint*, a popular hangout for U of I students. John told him it was open until the wee hours of the morning. Herb wondered if there was an intended double meaning to the diner's name, but he smelled no weed when he walked in, only coffee and grease. He sat at a small table near the window. He hoped a chair would offer more support to his tired back than a booth. No matter where he sat, there were only two color choices - black and gold or gold and black vinyl. Glancing at his watch, he mumbled, "Good thing I called Paul to tell him not to wait up." A weary waitress in a stained apron and a crooked name tag plunked down his hamburger and milk. She probably didn't get many tips from the student crowd. She looked more tired than he felt, and he resolved to leave her a good tip. Chewing his dry hamburger, Herb pulled out the borrowed paper back. It was an easy read, but grief was anything but easy. Herb tried to concentrate but loud talk from the adjoining booth intruded on his thoughts, so he put his book down, watched and listened.

Herb turned his chair so he could see them better. The one closest was tall and bony, with an Adam's apple that bobbed up and down when he talked. Next to him was a long-haired, full-bearded guy in a black 'Save Our Planet' t-shirt. He had the loudest voice. A mousey guy with thinning hair and a scraggly beard sat in the corner. Across the table were two women. A dishwater blonde with no makeup and thick glasses sat beside a redhead with a turned-up nose and a head which seemed too big for her small body.

After a minute of eavesdropping, Herb knew they were University students. Hearing them discuss dissertation committees and research projects convinced him they were grad students. They complained vigorously and disagreed frequently, but seemed unified in their disdain for Hawkeye home football weekends.

The blonde said, "It's such a mess on Saturdays, with the drunks and the traffic jams. I'd go back to New Jersey, if I could."

"Unfortunately," the tall one said, "I'm an Iowan and I've put up with this Iowa football crap my whole life!"

Mr. Save-the-Planet shrugged, "I could care less. We better buckle down and get ready for Thursday's big country tour."

Someone asked, "Where we going?"

"West Branch," the blonde said.

"Where's that?" the Californian asked.

The Iowa native answered, "Ten miles east, just off Interstate 80. West Branch is the quintessential small Iowa town except for its claim to fame ...." The four gave him blank stares. He lectured them, "You guys don't know, do you? Herbert Hoover, the 31st President of the US of A, was born there!"

"You majoring in trivia?" the redhead asked. "Who cares about the hometown of a failed president. Didn't Hoover lead the US of A into the Great Depression?"

The Iowan started to defend Hoover, but the guy in the corner ordered, "Hey, let's get this back on track."

"Thank you, O fearless leader!" the full-bearded one said. "You may have named us 'The Lab Rats' and you may be the only doctoral student and have seniority, but you're not our boss."

The redhead said, "Boys, stop fighting." She pulled out her laptop. "Dr. Sanders is requiring these three upcoming field trips to promote the University of Iowa."

"What does Sanders know about Iowa? She's a New Yorker," the blonde said. "The university hired her to whack budgets and grow research grants. We have to put on our public relations faces and help her court Iowa's fat cat investors. So, this week we go to a West Branch dairy farm. Next week it's a turkey processing plant in West Liberty...."

"We know the schedule," the redhead responded. "The third week, we visit the Quaker Oats plant in Cedar Rapids. All Iowa stuff. Supposedly Iowa State is doing a better job than we are of appealing to Iowa's rich business donors. Dr. Sanders said as much in her August memo. We evidently have to prove ourselves to these Iowa rubes or our research will be trimmed away like fat from a pork chop."

The doctoral student in the corner launched into a passionate tirade, "This is important to me! Sanders can ruin my life. I'm on the firing line. If I don't play nice with Sanders, my future is trashed. This is make or break; life or death!"

The tall Iowan interrupted, "Hey, cool it, man! We're all under the gun. We all depend on that big research grant. Who knows what our new east coast department chair will tell us on the 13th?"

"They brought her in to shake things up," the redhead added. "Lots of research grants expire December 31. Ours included."

'Save-the-planet' bellowed out, "The grant was supposed to be renewed. We don't need any more pressures on top of our deadlines, papers and tests!" A flood of personal woes gushed out.

They agreed, "It's life and death for all of us every time!"

Herb Lovejoy left his tip and stood. Fingering the new pack of business calling cards in his pocket, he stepped over to the students' booth and made an impulsive offer, "If anyone needs to talk about life and death stuff, I'm just over at the hospital. Hope your research goes well." Three students took his card. Herb paid his bill, waved goodbye to the table of students and ran out into the rain, unable to dodge the drops. 'Grad students aren't the only ones dealing with life and death.'

CHAPTER TEN:
Newcomers

Wednesday, September 5, 2001

The relentless rain depressed Jerry Kerr. He slogged through a sea of mud doing his morning farm chores. 'I ought to be happy. The vet came yesterday and helped old number 230 deliver a live heifer calf. The old gal is doing well and my production dynasty might continue for another generation. Corn crop looks good and the rain won't last forever. Next year we'll probably be begging for it.' When he got back to the house, he slumped into his mud-room chair and pulled off his boots.

"A penny for your thoughts?" asked his wife Marilyn.

"Don't waste your money… just feeling sorry for myself. We're running out of silage and this infernal rain never ends. You're lucky. You get to leave the mud and work inside all day."

Marilyn said, "Yes, I get to trade a grouchy husband for a batch of nervous new students."

Jerry grunted, "How many today?"

"Six. But I'm ready for them." She put on her raincoat and left with a parting remark, "By the way, when you come to town to have coffee and gossip with your buddies at McDonalds, I'll be in the trenches guiding America's next generation. Cheer up, Groucho!"

"Last name's Kerr, not Marx," he retorted. She hoped it made him feel better.

Marilyn beat the buses to West Branch High. Even after thirty years, she cherished quiet prep time before the opening bell. She sat at the head of her conference table and spread the transfer student folders out in front of her - two new juniors on the left, four seniors on the right. She re-read the files and was again impressed by the New York transfer. Kelly Sanders stuck out as a whiz in science and chemistry and was top in her class. The counselor laid out the folders on the table, so she could peek at the names. Today should be easy enough. Last week she had met seventy freshmen at once. Not so easy. She was glad that she remembered faces.

Marilyn had sketched her way through Ottumwa High School in southern Iowa and enrolled as an art major at The University of Iowa, before switching to elementary education. She had an artist's knack for noticing shapes and had a reputation for never forgetting a face. Her friends would be ticked if they knew she saw animals in their faces - elephants, gazelles, leopards, lizards, moose, monkeys, turtles, hounds and deer. She once told her husband Jerry that he looked and acted like a bulldog. She didn't tell anyone else about her facial obsession. She knew the usual teacher memory tricks, but preferred connecting each student with an animal's face.

'Wonder which part of the zoo I'll visit today?' she mused. Marilyn went to the door to call in the gang of six who sat nervously on folding chairs in the hallway. She invited them in and asked them to sit. "Please use a sharpie and write your first name on one of the disposable name tags. One student refused the magic marker and wrote her name with a No. 2 pencil. Two guys competed for the sloppiest name tag award. Both deserved to win. One girl's lettering was neat, but her name was smaller than a postage stamp. Two seniors made readable tags. Paul used big letters for his short name.

Kelly printed her name with a red marker and outlined it in blue. The flair appealed to the artist in Marilyn.

"Let's go around the table and tell our full names." Half of the students winced, preferring to keep their middle names a secret. "Also tell us where you're transferring from. I'll start. I'm Marilyn Anne Kerr, West Branch guidance counselor."

"Where'd you transfer from?" one scribbler asked.

"The University of Iowa," Marilyn said.

Not to be outdone, the other scribbler quipped, "I'm a Cyclone fan!"

"How about you?" she asked curtly. "Where are you from?"

He mumbled that he had moved from nearby Wilton.

Marilyn tagged him as a sleepy hound dog. She turned to the chemistry brain across the table, "Kelly, you're next."

"My name is Kelly Mae Sanders. I went to school in New Yawk City." Marilyn thought, 'Wildcat? Cheetah? Lioness?' She settled on Lioness.

"What about you, Paul?" the counselor asked.

"Paul Herbert Lovejoy". The first scribbler, when he heard the name, threw Paul an imaginary kiss and winked at Kelly.

Paul ignored the predictable response. "We just moved here from Joliet, Illinois." Marilyn thought the Lovejoy boy seemed like a sweet kid. A lamb didn't do him justice, but his gentleness pushed her thoughts there. A handsome young ram image might fit better. Her mind jumped the tracks, 'The lion and the lamb are sitting beside each other.' She remembered the rest of Sunday's sermon text from Isaiah, 'The lion shall lie down with the lamb.' She chided herself, 'The bible isn't talking about that kind of lying down!' The church bible lesson had been about how God wants to make peace and bring justice; even enemies like lions and lambs can be at peace with each other. But she had made a different connection between the New York girl and the Illinois boy. 'What am I thinking?'

After introductions, Marilyn handed them a tri-fold pamphlet, "Being the Best We Can Be." She summarized the school's behavioral wish-list, saw the clock and knew she was running out of time. She sprinted through her, 'How to adjust to a new school speech', "Keep your class schedule and map of the school campus handy...." Kelly wondered why anyone in such a small place would need a map. The junior transfer from Wilton thought the school was just the right size but was glad for the map. The scribblers didn't care. It was their senior year.

She concluded, unconsciously shifting to her counselor's voice, "It's not easy being the new kid on the block. Try to see this as an opportunity to grow. You'll be happier and make others happier if you make friends - new friends in a new place."

'Sounds like my dad,' Paul thought, as the bell sounded.

Walking into the hallway, Kelly raised her eyebrows and her voice, "Weren't those profound and amazing bits of advice! Wow. I'd have missed Iowa's Oprah if I'd stayed in New York." Paul was embarrassed by how loud she was but laughed anyway to try and impress her. After lunch in the Commons, their paths crossed again in the 2:00 p.m. Family Life and Consumer Science class. When they walked into the Home Economics Room, Kelly was reminded of her mistake. She'd signed up for all the 'science' courses in the West Branch school syllabus, not realizing what consumer science was. 'What science is there in Home Economics?' she thought. The teacher brought the newest students up to speed and updated the class on the next day's visit to a dairy farm. Kelly winced and whispered to Paul, "A farm tour? Oh, I forgot to unpack my bib overalls!"

He shrugged, "I don't know the dress code."

Kelly raised her hand and asked, "Why does a family life science class have to go to a dairy farm?"

The teacher answered, "Well... it's an annual class tradition here. As consumers, we need to know how our food is grown and processed...we need to know what makes it safe to eat or drink."

Kelly taunted the teacher again, "Why do we need a field trip? Isn't this school already in the middle of a corn field?"

Paul whispered, "We might learn something; discover the farm dress code or meet some nice cows."

"Cows are animals, aren't they? I am an animal lover."

The guy behind her overheard what she said, leaned forward and spoke with a throaty Elvis imitation, "Babe, I'm a real animal!"

She turned around and glared at the crew-cut, letter-jacket-wearing flirt, "I'd prefer spending time with real animals, rather than dumb football jocks pretending to be bulls or bears." Paul winced, not wanting Kelly to know how much he loved football.

CHAPTER ELEVEN:
Hospital Humor

Thursday, September 6, 2001

Chaplain Herb Lovejoy got to the hospital half an hour early to check on little Billy Griffin. He hurried through the hospital lobby to the elevator, punched the up arrow and drummed his fingers on the silver doorway. "Come on. Come on." Herb knew he shouldn't be so invested in the NICU baby. The life-and-death struggle of this tiny baby had hooked something deep within him. Was he remembering Brenda's struggles to give birth to their son Paul? Herb replayed memories of Paul's birth. He had been full-term, but it was a difficult breech delivery. Paul's life was touch-and-go for a few hours.

The elevator door finally opened and Herb stepped in. He'd noticed that most hospital elevator passengers looked grim-faced or exhausted; too few looked relieved or hopeful. Herb wanted to be in the second group. He wasn't disappointed when he walked into the NICU waiting room. Last night's gloom had lifted a bit for the Griffins. Little Billy had survived the latest crisis.

Terri told him, "They're supposed to do another big test this morning, but we can go see him first. They say I can't hold him yet, but he's alive. I've waited for 39 years to hold this baby. I can wait a few more days. Would you go in with us? Sorry, chaplain, I forgot your name."

"That's OK, It's Herb Lovejoy. I'd be happy to go with you."

Terri led the way to the nursery, followed by husband Bill and Herb. They suited up in disposable hospital gowns and blue booties. The protective wardrobe was completed with latex gloves and the required face masks. A nurse cleared them to go into the nursery. Once through the sealed door, another nurse led them into the emergency room for babies. She said, "He's in the third bed." The bed was a clear plastic box, like the tubs you'd buy at a big box store. They saw a license plate sized nametag on the front of the bed-GRIFFIN, William Jr., No.75-66324-9, born 9-2-2001.

Little Billy, not much bigger than his father's beefy right hand, was nestled in what looked like a pillow. A tiny tube was taped to his nose to pump oxygen into his weak lungs. The nurse said, "Learning to breathe is one of the hardest things for preemies. We cover his eyes, so they aren't damaged when he gets light therapy to prevent jaundice." Herb remembered that preemies had to fight several wars at once: lung failure, potential brain damage, infections and heart problems. Male babies had higher fatality rates. The nurse explained more of the tubes, "The pic line lets us give him meds without using needles. We'll do all we can to keep him comfortable while we're helping him get better. The first four days are crucial and your son Billy is holding his own."

Back in the waiting room, Terri Griffin thanked Herb profusely. "Just being here last night helped us more than you'll ever know! Our folks got here, so we're not so alone. I wish you could have met them, but they're downstairs getting something to eat. They're almost as tired as we are. We need all the help we can get. Would you pray for us?"

"Certainly," Herb responded, "What would you like us to pray for?" He knew in his gut what they needed, but was trained to ask.

"Pray that Billy lives... and can be a normal boy," Terri said.

Herb prayed with them and then hurried to the spiritual care team meeting. He made it with 30 seconds to spare. Spiritual Director Elaine Armstrong welcomed him and introduced the team, "You met John yesterday. You two can brief us on your NICU visits later. Across the table is Father Patrick O'Neil. He's especially appreciated by our Catholic patients." Herb thought the priest looked as young as his son Paul.

Elaine said, "Last, but not least, I want you to meet Connie Baughman. Her specialty is grief and loss." Herb shook hands with the brunette with striking brown eyes. Baughman had an uncanny resemblance to his wife Brenda. Was it her eyes? She wore a clerical collar, but no ring.

After reports on Tuesday's visits, the director gave them assignments for the afternoon, "I want to send you out with two centering thoughts. First, from Thomas More, 'Earth has no sorrow that Heaven cannot heal.'" Herb hoped it was true. "And from Mother Teresa, 'The biggest disease today is not leprosy or tuberculosis, but rather the feeling of being unwanted, uncared for and deserted by everybody. The greatest evil is the lack of love and charity.'"

Chaplain Baughman affirmed, "Thanks, Elaine, for the usual good words." The two women seemed to respect each other.

The chaplains spent the afternoon visiting patients and didn't see each other again until four hours later. They had agreed to eat together in the main cafeteria. Connie Baughman brought a brown bag and found a corner table for them. Herb and Father O'Neil got trays and went through the cafeteria line. John walked in last, laughing so hard, he almost spilled his soup. "You won't believe what happened to me today. I was visiting a patient recovering from surgery, when his next door neighbor barged into the room. My jaw dropped to the floor when he leaned over the hospital bed and told the patient, 'Hal, you don't look so good. What'd they do to you?'

'Took out my gall bladder,' said the patient.

'Sorry to hear that, neighbor. Both my brother and my old army buddy died right after that surgery. But you have survived…at least so far.' The visitor saw my clerical collar and asked, 'Hey Reverend, you here to do last rites?' I was too stunned to tell him I was a Lutheran."

Father O'Neil blurted, "Wish I'd been there, I'd have given that insensitive visitor his last rites. Hospital rooms should be sanctuaries of dignity!"

"I agree about the need for dignity, Padre, but hospital rooms can sometimes be funny places," Chaplain Baughman offered.

Six eyebrows jumped.

"What do you mean?"

"I once walked in on a family circled around an elderly man in Post Op. He seemed comatose and near death. I assumed the four agitated couples were his children and their spouses. You could hear them all the way to the nurses' station. 'He's all but gone! Phil, did you finalize those funeral plans?'

'I can't do that until you two agree on the casket.'

'Who's going to contact Aunt Bess?' another asked. The conversation heated up.

Then their father sat up and rasped out, 'I'm not dead yet!'

"Remember," Connie said, "even a patient who looks totally comatose can often hear what we say."

"Good reminder," Herb said as he finished his grilled chicken salad. "But we should be wary of believing everything a patient says. I once visited an old church saint who was having a heart valve replaced. I was shocked by what she said when I visited her in the recovery room, 'Don't believe them, pastor. The terrorists are in the building. Everyone will be killed. But I can stop them.' She lifted her arm. 'See this red button. That's what I push to stop them!'

I couldn't believe my ears. I'd never heard her say anything like that in the years I'd known her."

"Was it the drugs?" O'Neil asked.

"Exactly! I went back three days later and she was her old self, asking about the church budget and if we'd fixed the women's toilet yet. She had no memory of the whole ordeal, but I won't forget it. I was so concerned that I called her surgeon. He told me, 'She's tough and has a strong will to survive.' When he talked to her about the surgery risks for an 86-year-old, she said, 'I bet you'll charge me whether I live or die.' The doc told me, 'I'm betting on her survival.' The doc was right. She's still living on the family farm."

"Doctors sometimes get it right," O'Neil said, through the last bite of his fish sandwich.

John asked, "Father O'Neil, you're eating fish on Thursdays?"

"Fish isn't just for Fridays anymore," O'Neil retorted.

"You are right. Doctors say fish is good for our hearts," John admitted.

Herb asked, "How was the soup, John?"

"Better than your heart-healthy salad," John said as he turned to Connie, "How were your veggies, Connie?"

She pushed her empty Tupperware bowl aside. "John, they are very good, I grew them myself."

Father O'Neil finished his sandwich. "We Irish Catholics like a good story, too. Let me tell you the one about a rabbi, priest and preacher who went into a hospital room at the same time…."

"I know the ending," John said.

"Let him finish, John," Connie scolded. "You aren't the only one with a sense of humor."

O'Neil continued, "…The three clerics were shocked to meet in a hospital room. The rabbi asked the patient, 'You called all three of us?'

'No. But I did check all the religious preference boxes on the registration form- Catholic, Protestant, Jewish,' the patient answered.

'Why check them all? Wouldn't one be enough?' the preacher asked.

'I wanted to cover all my bets, so I checked them all. If I don't make it through surgery, I have five million bucks to leave someone! Who can guide this compulsive gambler to Heaven?'

The rabbi declined, 'You can't buy God's favor.'

The preacher said, 'My church doesn't believe in gambling!'

The priest stepped to the bed, 'Welcome, brother! We have bingo every Thursday night.'"

John chuckled, "That's a new version of the old story. By the way, didn't I see on the roster that there's another gambler being prepped for surgery who needs a priestly visit!"

"Sorry," O'Neil said, "I'm not rushing off and leaving my chocolate chip cookies behind."

"Would you share one?" John asked.

"Take one. Grace be upon you… even if you don't laugh at my jokes."

Conner took the cookie, "Bless me, O father…."

All four guffawed.

Father O'Neil said, "Whoever said, 'Laughter is the best medicine' got it right!"

Conner instructed, "That phrase was coined by protestant preacher Henry Ward Beecher. You Catholics aren't the only ones with great quotes."

Father O'Neil smiled, "There's still only one Mother Teresa!"

CHAPTER TWELVE:
Farm Tour

Thursday, September 6, 2001

Cars, buses and pickups crowded the Kerr Dairy Farm's gravel driveway. A blue and white tent, angled between the house and the old barn, billowed in the wind. The annual Tri-County Dairy Tour was about to begin. A man, looking out of his element, stood awkwardly, tightened his striped blue tie and tapped the portable microphone. It screeched as he began, "On behalf of the State Dairy Association, I want to welcome all of you, especially the West Branch High School's Family and Consumer Science class and the University of Iowa neurotoxin research team. Thanks to the Cedar and Johnson County Pork Producers Associations for our delicious lunch and to the Kerr's for hosting this event." The crowd of farmers and students, applauded politely. He continued, "We're sorry about today's muddy conditions, but we're glad you're here. The Kerrs will guide your tour of their operation. Mrs. Kerr, will you take half our guests out to the cow barn? We've provided you with protective blue plastic covers to put over your shoes. These will protect the cows from anything you might carry in and will protect you from tracking anything smelly back into your vehicles." Two high school boys pinched their noses in mock disgust. As Marilyn's group headed toward the barns, the suit made another introduction, "Jerry Kerr will show you the milking operation. Will you follow him to the milk house?"

A high school senior whispered loudly, "Is that like a gingerbread house made with milk?" He intended to be heard and Jerry Kerr didn't ignore him.

"In answer to the question from the nut gallery, the milk house is made of concrete, wood and steel, not gingerbread. It's where we 'house' the milk. The parlor isn't grandma's sitting room; it's where we milk the cows. You'll need to put your plastic blue slippers on before we go inside. That's to protect our pristine milking environment from your germs. The floor is clean enough to eat off of. This way! I'll show you where your milk comes from."

A few teens were genuinely interested, but most were just glad to get out of school. This was especially true for the seniors with early onset senioritis. The University of Iowa research team asked technical questions. Kerr was surprised at their interest in details about his work - when he milked the cows, who helped him and when he slept. "Not enough sleeping time," he answered. "But I do have a full-time hired man who does the morning milking and cleans up. He also oversees raising the calves. My wife Marilyn does most of our bookwork. I couldn't do everything by myself." A grad student asked about lighting, security and sanitation procedures.

The other tour group followed Mrs. Kerr. Kelly Sanders walked gingerly in her crinkly shoe covers and caught up with Mrs. Kerr, "Don't farms always have dogs?"

Marilyn answered, "Usually. But we lost our German Shepherd, Jake, last year and we were so attached that we haven't had the heart to replace him." Marilyn's attention was distracted by a farmer on her left who had a German Shepherd face and a U of I student who looked like a mouse with a tuft of beard. She had already identified the wildcat and the ram, a bear, a hound dog, a beaver and two cats. She banished her compulsion by starting her dairy tour spiel. "Do you know what our black and white cows are called?"

"Cop cows!" the senior class clown answered.

"No," Marilyn said, "They are 'Holstein-Friesian.' Holsteins are the most popular dairy cows in the USA."

Kelly did a 360, "Where are the cows?"

"They're in the barn, Miss Sanders, this way!" Thirty students and neighbors followed Mrs. Kerr up a slope into a big barn with two rows of free stalls where the cows slept. "Watch your step, the floor can be slippery. This is our confinement barn."

Kelly thought, 'Isn't that another word for prison?' She saw huge cows jammed into small spaces and forced to live on concrete.

The tour group walked by two tall silos and along a row of pine trees to reach a cluster of little white houses where the baby calves lived. Marilyn called them 'calf hutches'. Each calf had a small wire cage out front. When they stepped out of the pines, the calves bolted, some crashed into the metal fence. One fell down. Kelly accused, "Is this all the space they get? There's not enough room for a hamster!" It looked like solitary confinement to her.

Marilyn responded, "These individual calf houses are the penthouses of calf-care." She could tell the answer didn't satisfy. "We used to raise them jammed together in a dark old barn."

Kelly responded, "At least then they could be together."

"They're happy, now. Kelly, go ahead and pet one of them."

The city girl reached over the fence toward a mostly black calf with a white diamond on the forehead. It licked her hand. Kelly was delighted, "She's almost as black as my lab. She's so cute!"

"When they're a few weeks older, we put heifer calves in groups of a dozen," Marilyn said.

"Heifers are girl cows," a farm boy explained for Kelly's benefit.

"What happens to the boy calves?" Kelly asked.

"We sell them to another farmer who raises veal calves," Marilyn said.

"Veal, like the meat people eat?"

"Yes."

41

"So they kill these cute babies so we can eat fancy meat?" Kelly was incensed.

Marilyn hadn't thought about it that way.

When the tour was over, Kelly stomped back to the bus and slid in next to Paul. "What's bugging you?" he asked.

"I'll tell you what! Did you see those cows jammed in behind bars? Mrs. Farmer lady said it was called, 'confinement.' Baby calves are in tiny jails and can hardly move. She's our guidance counselor and ought to know better than to mistreat animals. If you can't trust someone with animals, how can you trust them with people? They kill the boy calves!" The more Kelly talked, the madder she got.

CHAPTER THIRTEEN:
Soar

Friday, September 7, 2001

By the time school ended the next day, Kelly had found several girls who agreed with her views about animal rights. She voiced a passion they secretly nursed. She was on a recruiting mission. Guys followed along like curious puppies, trying to stay in the good graces of the girls. Paul figured that Kelly wouldn't like you if you didn't like dogs. He was glad he did.

On the afternoon bus ride home from West Branch, she surprised him, "Going to the football game tonight?"

"Sure! Want to go with me?"

"Meet me at the game, you can drive me home," she said with a glint in her eye. She was also a flirt.

That evening, Paul arrived at the stadium just before the kickoff and scrambled up the bleachers looking for Kelly. The announcer said, "Welcome to the *Little Rose Bowl*, home of the West Branch Bears, reigning Cedar Valley District 6 champs. Tonight, we face-off with our arch-rivals, the West Liberty Comets." The West Branch crowd roared; they were used to winning. Head football coach Butch Pedersen had done amazing things in his eighteen years at West

Branch, including a record 62 consecutive wins from 1990 through 1997 and three state championships. Paul spotted Kelly in a cluster of chatting girls on the bleachers above the 40- yard line. He lost sight of her when the crowd erupted in a volcano of waving arms.

Football cleats clattered on the pavement as the West Branch team charged down onto the field. Paul edged his way through the excited crowd and stood beside Kelly. She gave him a smile and returned to her conversation about fighting animal abuse. A guy, a couple of rows up, overheard Kelly's animal rights pitch and said, "West Branch Bears don't need no protecting."

Kelly's response was drowned out by the cheerleaders belting out the West Branch fight song. After the song, all attention turned to the field. In the stands, red and black home team colors dominated the royal blue and white of the visitors.

The West Branch Bears kicked off and the West Liberty Comets ran the ball back to the one- yard line. The runner shredded the Bear defenders. On the next play, the visitors scored. West Branch tried running the ball, but was held to two yards in three attempts. West Liberty took the punt and ran it back for another touchdown. The initially rowdy *Little Rose Bowl* home crowd was silenced. When West Branch's second pass attempt was intercepted, Paul leaned over and told Kelly, "West Liberty is out for blood and revenge." But Kelly had already lost what little interest she had in the game. She was focused on recruiting her own team of reformers and told a girl in front of them, "All animals have rights and feelings: cats, cows, elephants and even bears."

By half-time, Bear fans felt abused and beaten-up. Last year they'd kicked off the season by beating West Liberty in a nail-biter and never lost a regular-season game. They were Champs! Hardcore fans could remember how West Branch once beat Clear Creek-Amana 81-0; the officials had to call off that game at halftime. But tonight was different. The fans grew restless in the second half and came to life only once, when senior Cody Klein took the ball in for their only touchdown. Disappointed Bears players slumped off the field after a 48-7 shellacking. Paul was almost glad he wasn't on the team.

Kelly poked him. Her mind was still riveted on animal abuse, "I just came up with the perfect name for our group! Get this - 'Society of Animal Rights' (S.O.A.R.)." Paul thought it was a good name. As the game crowd milled around, Kelly gathered her SOAR team together for a final huddle near the concession stand, sipping drinks, talking and laughing. A circle of guys surrounded Kelly's five all-girl SOAR team. Paul enjoyed being caught up in the slipstream of her passion. He was afraid she wanted to wait around and recruit some members of the football team. Paul didn't want that to happen. Enough guys were already hanging around. "Hey Kelly, you ready to go home?"

"Yeah, I better go. My folks will expect the weekly report on my educational experiences and I've been away from Darth too long!"

Paul drove her home. His jaw dropped when he saw her log home. It could have filled half the West Branch football field. She asked, "What do you think of our big house in the little woods? He was beginning to appreciate her sense of humor. Kelly gave him a quick peck on the cheek, jumped out of the car and ran to the house. She was eager to tell her parents all about SOAR. Watching her sprint, Paul wasn't sure he could keep up with her, but knew he wanted to try.

After dropping her off, he pulled into his own driveway and parked near the rickety picket fence poking up through the weeds and brush. The old farm house was about the size of Kelly's garage. Paul was ashamed, then remembered an old saying, "It's not what you've got that counts, but what you do with what you've got." When he opened the squeaky door, his father waved two Iowa football tickets, "We're going to the game - Happy Birthday!" Paul gave his dad a high five.

CHAPTER FOURTEEN:
Murder

Saturday, September 8, 2001

Dr. Ruth Sanders gathered up her briefcase and laptop, kissed her husband and walked through the kitchen. Daughter Kelly complained, "You have to work again? It's Saturday!"

"Sorry," Ruth said. Then she impulsively asked, "Why don't you come to the office with me? You like the lab and we could do lunch."

"Mom, it's game day, the traffic will be terrible."

Glancing at her watch, Ruth replied, "You're right. But if we leave now we'll miss the Hawkeye-mania. We can drive back during the game and avoid them again."

Kelly knew she needed to get away from her obsession with SOAR. "OK. Lab and lunch will be fine. I've had enough football for this week. Do I have to get dressed up?"

Ruth looked her over. "Jeans and tennis shoes will do, won't be many people in the office today."

Traffic was normal until they reached Iowa City. The diehard Hawkeye fans were already rushing in to claim the best parking spots and ready to do some tailgating. Threading through the thickening traffic, Dr. Sanders explained her work urgency, "I wasn't planning to go in today, but the autopsy results came in late yesterday."

"What autopsy?" Kelly asked.

"Didn't I tell you that one of my research professors died Tuesday?"

Kelly said, "This is the first I've heard about it. Why an autopsy? Do Iowans do one for everybody who dies?"

"No," her mother answered. "But it was a sudden suspicious death, so one was ordered." As they pulled into her coveted reserved parking space, she added, "It was not natural causes - apparently a poisoning."

Kelly released her seatbelt, "Suicide or murder?"

"I'm no detective but it sounds like murder to me. Whatever, it means extra work for me. Today, I have to figure out what to do with Egstrom's classes. Also I need to meet with one of my lab research leaders. Why don't we start there? Hopefully it won't take long. You can tag along and scope out the lab." Kelly followed her mother down to the laboratory. The teenager had always loved lab visits. Today was no exception. They walked into the world of microscopes, vials, computers and chemicals.

A face popped up from behind a computer screen. "Dr Sanders?"

Ruth answered, "Yes, Daniel. I wanted to brief you on the department's plan for evaluating your research project." She continued explaining as she walked across the room to his computer station. He stood awkwardly.

Kelly thought the guy had a funny look on his face. Not just the scraggly attempt at a beard but something else. She soon lost interest and poked around the lab, fascinated by the latest high-tech research gadgets. She paid little attention to their conversation, until her mother said, "Kelly. Let's go upstairs."

The smells of the lab were replaced by the odor of new carpet. Ruth Sander's office was worthy of a corporate executive. It was the corner power office with a window view of the Iowa River. The desk was a rich mahogany that matched the carpet. A corner table overflowed with books and stacks of scientific journals.

Ruth pointed to them, "Why don't you browse through those journals, while I answer emails and make some phone calls?"

Kelly sat down and thumbed through several journals. She pulled a journal from the bottom of the stack, opened it and scanned the table of contents page. A headline grabbed her. "Botulinum Toxin as a Biological Weapon." She turned to page 1059 and read how foodborne botulinum could pose a significant public health threat. Poisoning the masses with a toxin. 'Scary,' she thought as she waded through the research and the threat warnings.

"Mom, have you seen this article by a Civilian Biodefense research group? You should read it. They warn that foods, even milk, could be poisoned by Botulinum Toxin and thousands might die. Wouldn't want terrorists to get hold of that stuff!"

"Kelly, I've seen similar articles. It's mostly headline-grabbing; the science is still a little thin. As matter of fact, we are using that same toxin in one of our research projects."

"Really. Can I see it?"

"If we have time before lunch, I'll take you down and show you."

Kelly said, "Let's hurry. All this talk about toxins poisoning our food really perks up my appetite."

Her mother asked, "Shall we go to the usual place?"

"O yeah!" Kelly said as she threw the journal back on the table. "And I'll still have mine with milk."

CHAPTER FIFTEEN:
Game Day

Saturday, September 8, 2001

A half-mile away in University of Iowa's Kinnick Stadium, Paul Lovejoy and his dad were not drinking milk, they were drinking cokes. It had been a great first half for the Hawkeyes, dominating Miami of Ohio from the first play. It was 24 to zip. The home crowd was whooping it up and guzzling it down. "Dad, go easy on the coke, or you'll have to take another trip to the head before the game is over."

"Good point. But the game seems pretty well over."

Paul shrugged. "You're probably right, given how Iowa is playing. That 52-yard pass from Kyle McCann to number 3 was a beauty. He threw two touchdown passes in nine minutes."

His father said, "And the Iowa defense sent Miami's freshman quarterback to the sidelines. Miami has slowed down Iowa's running game but the Hawks keep throwing the bombs."

The Lovejoy's were fast becoming Hawkeye fans. It was a thundering crowd, a rare cloudless sunny day and they had great seats at the ten-yard line. But one dark ominous cloud hung on the horizon – the accident. Tomorrow would be the second anniversary of the wreck that killed Paul's mother and his sister. September 9, 1999 was forever burned into their memories. Both needed the guy-escape of a football game.

Half-time entertainment ended and Herb leaned over. "Paul, I was thinking about your first day at school and wondered how you're doing in the friend department? As bad as you feared? As good as I'd promised?"

Paul shrugged. "Yes and no. I've found a couple of friends. Kelly is the one I know best."

"Is Kelly a guy or a gal?" Herb asked.

"Girl."

"Cute?"

"Yeah. Out of my league, but way too young for you!" Paul laughed.

Herb said, "Don't underestimate yourself."

The second half started and everything kept going Iowa's way. Sophomore tight end Dallas Clark, a former walk-on linebacker, caught two long touchdown passes and took them into the end zone. As if carefully orchestrated, after the extra point, the crowd turned together toward the scoreboard in the south end zone. 44 to 0. Even Iowa's most ardent 'run up the score' fans were not surprised when Coach Ferentz took his starters out of the game and sent in his second string. The crowd's attention began to drift toward next week's big game with in-state-rival, Iowa State. Fans got a wake-up call when Miami's freshman quarterback, Ben Roethlisberger brushed off Iowa tacklers, punched through the defense and galloped 80 yards for a touchdown. Three minutes later, he fired a 56-yard touchdown pass. That sobered the Hawkeyes. The rambunctious crowd was quieted. Paul exclaimed, "Coach Ferentz has to do something to stop Roethlisberger." As if following Paul's advice, Ferentz sent his starting defensive string back into the game. Iowa's stellar defense slowed Miami's momentum. It ended well for Iowa, with a 44-19 victory.

On the way back to the car, they talked about Iowa and Miami coaching styles and strategies. "A team needs to know what to do and when to do it." Paul observed.

"You got it. They also need to know where they're going."

Paul walked silently for half a block before saying, "Dad I'm not sure I know where my life is going. In junior high, I thought about following your steps into the ministry...."

"But not now?" Herb asked.

"You don't seem to know where you're going either. You and Mom always talked about the importance of college, but what good has it done you? You had seven years of college; you're almost fifty and still don't seem to know what to do with your life!"

Herb didn't have an answer and wondered how a single dad who doesn't know where he's going himself can guide a son.

They got into the Toyota. Unanswered questions traveled with them all the way back to West Branch. As they pulled into their rutted driveway, Paul broke the silence. "Thanks for the game. It was the best thing that's happened in two years!"

CHAPTER SIXTEEN:
1984 Revisited

Sometime, 1984

"**B**oy, shut that thing off and get in here," Danny's father scolded. Watching a single Saturday morning cartoon was considered a terrible waste of time. His father had a one-word plan for Danny's life – study, study, study. 'Be smart, get smarter!' Danny, a nine-year-old 4th grader, was reading at 10th grade level and tested off the charts in everything except relating to peers. But his father wasn't satisfied.

Danny rushed into the study, hoping to please his dad. The house smelled of old books. Books were stacked to the ceiling, some on shelves, many in precarious piles, leaving a narrow entry-exit pathway. "Slow down, boy." On good days he was called 'Danny boy', but most days he was just 'boy'. Brushing aside stacks of notes, he picked up two books. "Here's your reading assignment for this week." Danny sagged under the weight of the two books - Darwin's *Origin of the Species* and Melville's *Moby Dick*.

"Focus on science but don't ignore the classics. The college crowd wants both. I expect you to excel at both! Give me your reviews next Saturday. Be prepared. George Orwell warned us in his classic *1984*, 'If you want a picture of the future, imagine a boot stomping on a human face.' He wrote that in 1949, the year I was born. Orwell's book haunts me. You know what year it is, don't you, boy?" He answered his own question, "1984. 1-9-8-4!"

Danny trudged back to his corner, burdened by the books and the impossibility of pleasing his father. There were no father-son small talks, no ball games, no affection and no affirmation. The only bonding times were Sunday afternoons when Danny enjoyed laboratory lessons and wild experiments in their empty garage. His father treated him like an apprentice, teaching him about Bunsen burners and test tubes, chemicals and biological agents. Periodic Table flash cards replaced LA Dodger baseball cards in Danny's world.

He tried, but no matter how well he did, it was not enough. "Boy, you're dumber than your mother. You are a sorry dumb runt!"

In February, his father got very agitated when he read about a discovery at UCLA's Medical Center, "This research was done by my college classmate, John Buster. We took a biology class together and I got the top grade." But comparing his achievements to his successful peer pushed his father closer to some inner precipice. He became increasingly gloomy and withdrawn.

Danny knew something was terribly wrong the Sunday his father growled, "Go back to the house. Get out of my lab!" There were no experiments that day. Danny wanted to beg him to come out of the dark garage, but didn't dare. On Monday, when he got home from school, his father was gone. Danny was bewildered and confused. His mother's explanation didn't help. It didn't matter. His father was gone. Danny never saw him again.

CHAPTER SEVENTEEN:
Attack

8:00 am. September 11, 2001

Counselor Marilyn Kerr welcomed the early birds to her home room. West Branch High students were having a bad week. They had not recovered from the terrible, horrible, very bad football day on Friday. There was none of the usual Tuesday morning chatter, except for newcomers Kelly Sanders and Paul Lovejoy. They sat together at the back of the room. An Iowa road map was unfolded in front of them. They were laughing at the map. Kerr thought about reprimanding the couple but got caught up in their conversation. "Where did they come up with these names?" Sanders asked. "Look at them, 'What Cheer?' Where's 'Cheer Up'?"

Lovejoy shook his head. "West Liberty is east of West Branch. At least North Liberty is north of them." He smiled

"Where is South Liberty? And where is East Branch? It must be closer to the Mississippi," she said as the principal's secretary burst into the room. "Turn on the TV!" 'What's happened?' Marilyn wondered. She switched on the TV behind her. Students gasped, eyes glued to the screen. The horror of 9/11's terror attack on America unfolded. Funny Iowa town names and disappointing football games were forgotten.

Marilyn's stomach knotted up. She was reliving the assassination of President John F. Kennedy. Nov. 22, 1963 was a day she could not forget. She had been in a senior educational theory class at U. of I. Two seats away, a guy who had smuggled a transistor radio into class interrupted the professor, "The President has been shot!"

'It's the same today,' Marilyn thought. The usual school sounds were hijacked by television reports and commentators. They owned every room in West Branch High for the rest of the day. Bears' football practices and Friday's game were cancelled.

Students jammed the commons/lunch room watching events unfold. Before the morning was over, she was overwhelmed by fearful students who had questions no guidance counselor could answer. Some, like Kelly Sanders, sat in mute shock. Senior boys talked about enlisting in the marines, scaring their already frightened girlfriends.

Marilyn realized, 'I can't handle this myself!'

CHAPTER EIGHTEEN:
War Again

8:31 am. September 11, 2001

Jerry Kerr wasn't sure he could stand another rainy week. He had to chop some corn, or he'd run out of feed. His last silo was almost empty. Saturday's sunny day was replaced by familiar steel grey clouds and spits of rain. Jerry was tired of working between storms. "I need more coffee." He walked to his office, made a fresh pot and turned on his TV.

The routine farm market report on corn price futures was interrupted by breaking news of explosions in New York City. 'Are we at war? Has New York been bombed? Not the Pentagon! It can't be happening!' He watched it all day. Seeing the same thing over and over again sickened him and so did the stream of speculation by the TV talking heads. They didn't know what it was like to be attacked. Jerry did. His past reared its ugly head and spewed out the old war poison - bullets and smoke; blood and death; fear and guilt. Buried Vietnam War experiences boiled to the surface. Jerry fought to breathe. His denim overalls morphed into battle fatigues covered with blood. Corporal J. F. Kerr was sinking fast. The Nam vet was shaking so hard he could barely dial the familiar Colorado number. He had to talk to his army buddy. 'Pick up. Come on Mike. Pick up!'

Kerr smelled cordite and felt elephant grass whip his face. He heard the chatter of gunfire, the whiz of bullets and the screams of the wounded. Snipers caught his unit in a deadly crossfire. After fifty hours of fighting, their bloodied greenhorn unit wallowed through the elephant grass on their way to be evacuated. But even crawling through the grass betrayed their positions and invited more bullets. The snipers were shooting from trees on both sides of the trail. They were pinned down and fired back wildly. A third of the Americans were cut down before the snipers could be neutralized. The explosions in New York and DC tore open old wounds. He was scrambling for his life and firing wildly. There was blood on his dirty uniform.

Farmer Jerry Kerr crawled out from under his office table clutching, not a rifle, but his telephone. A familiar voice sounded in his ear. Pulling himself back into his chair, he gasped, "Mike, Mike, it's me Jerry, J.F.K. Yeah, I saw the news. I'm freaked out. Damned TV explosions forced me back to Nam and la Drang! I thought I was going to die."

They talked for an hour about the fateful November 17, 1965 battle in the Highlands of Vietnam. Jerry's sanity returned as he listened to his buddy.

"No, Mike, I can't forget la Drang as much as I want to. We almost bought the farm that day!" Mike used his usual humor to try to ease Jerry's pain.

"Yes, Mike, I did buy the farm here in Iowa. That's why I'm up to my eyeballs in debt and mud." They talked about old times and friends who died in the fighting during U.S. Operation Silver Bayonet. Battle bonds were deep, but Jerry concealed war secrets, even from Mike. He kicked off his boots, propped his feet on a plastic bucket of tools under the table and listened to Mike's stories.

Jerry laughed, "No Mike. They don't call me J.F.K back here. That's the moniker you guys hung on me. Here they just call me 'Jerry' or 'the Kerr boy'"

"You don't remember my full name? Jerry Franklin Kerr".

"I'm no Kennedy, Mike, but you can still call me J.F.K. if you want to." Kerr never told hometown friends about his service nickname. He was a staunch Republican and would never hear an end to the ribbing about his being a Kennedy who slept with a Marilyn. Wife Marilyn thought the J.F.K. nickname was silly. She told him he didn't look at all like a Kennedy.

Calmed down, Jerry signed off, "Mike. You take care and stay out of the elephant grass."

"Yes, I'll say hello to my Marilyn. Keep in touch." Kerr hung up, wondering why he still couldn't tell Mike about what really happened in Nam.

CHAPTER NINETEEN:
Reports

9:07 am. September 11, 2001

Chaplain Lovejoy enjoyed a relaxed drive to work listening to a favorite CD. He was puzzled when he walked into the University Hospitals lobby. People were clustered around TVs watching what looked like a war movie. CNN was reporting, "The South Tower of New York's World Trade Center has collapsed." Herb saw the proud 110-story building fall into a pile of rubble, sending up a ten-story plume of dust, smoke and debris. Images jumped and jerked as crowds tried to outrun the expanding cloud. How could such an architectural marvel collapse like a child's sand castle? CNN news cut to an engineer explaining why the steel structure fell when struck by one airplane.

"An airplane?" Herb blurted out.

"An hour ago, a jetliner hit the South Tower. It just collapsed," a nurse responded. "The North Tower was struck by another airliner at 7:42 this morning. They think terrorists hijacked the planes." Herb was stunned. He'd visited New York's Twin Towers during his senior year in high school. It seemed impossible to imagine the New York skyline with one of them missing.

Someone turned up the TV. CNN's consulting expert said, "The WTC was designed to withstand winds in excess of 200 miles an hour, not the tremendous heat generated by an airliner loaded with jet fuel. It was more than the structural steel frame could take."

"At this time, we know that four jets were hijacked, two crashed into the twin towers, one into the Pentagon and one in rural Pennsylvania," the anchor reported.

Herb couldn't believe it. He spent the rest of the day going room-to-room, visiting patients and watching reruns of the 102 minutes that changed the world.

A grisly World War II veteran wanted to disconnect his IV's and trade his hospital gown for his old Army Uniform, "This is Pearl Harbor all over again! They'll pay!" The old patriot had fighting fire in his eyes but his cancer-riddled body wouldn't follow orders. Another massive cloud of smoke mushroomed on the TV screen the veteran was watching. The weakened North Tower fell to its death and took hundreds of people with it. Herb stared at it with horror. Airports were closed and all commercial flights cancelled. Lower Manhattan was being evacuated. Herb didn't have answers for the explosion of questions he heard from patients and their families. "Why? "Who did this?"

From the television screen, Utah's Senator Orrin Hatch answered, "…This looks like the signature of Osama bin Laden… he may be behind this."

Lovejoy hurried along the fourth floor corridor. 'One more visit before lunch.' Except for the comatose or sedated, most patients were glued to the tube. Herb stood in the doorway for a minute, not wanting to interrupt the President, "Freedom, itself, was attacked this morning by a faceless coward. And freedom will be defended."

"May I come in?" Herb thought he'd walked into Field Museum's Mummy room. The patient was trussed up with both legs and one arm in casts.

She motioned with her free hand, "Please do. Are you a doctor?"

"No. I'm Chaplain Lovejoy."

"Chaplain, America could sure use God's help right about now."

Herb offered a prayer for America's recovery and for hers.

Americans were encouraged by the stories of heroism rising from the ashes of tragedy. Patients repeated stories of heroic firefighters who gave their lives rescuing others. Acts of New York heroism were celebrated by Iowa patients. Herb heard a scattered applause with each televised testimony. But bad news kept coming. The smoldering 47 story World Trade Center building collapsed. The entire complex was gone.

Herb thought about New York's chaos and terror as he drove home through Iowa's gentle rolling fields. Death and destruction had enveloped the country, but determined Iowa farmers were chopping corn silage. Here in the Midwest there were no war zone mushroom clouds of smoke and death, just tiny plumes from diesel tractors and small belches of corn dust from choppers. The rusty patches of soybeans, ripening corn and green alfalfa offered peace and tranquility. Herb rolled down his window and breathed it in.

CHAPTER TWENTY:
Homefront

7:00 pm. September 11, 2001

A few miles north, Stephen, Ruth and Kelly Sanders finished a tense dinner. New York City loomed large in their rural Iowa house. Ruth had spent the afternoon trying in vain to phone daughter Marie back in New York, "Stephen, I can't reach her."

"Ruth, I heard that millions of calls jammed the phone lines," he replied. "Marie is fine and will get hold of us when she can. We just have to be patient."

Kelly sat in icy silence.

Stephen and Ruth had also failed to reach any former co-workers or friends in Upper Manhattan's Weill Medical College. They shared an unspoken conviction that Kelly's best friend's parents, who worked on the 90th floor of the South Tower, were dead. Both avoided eye contact with Kelly. Terror images faded from the TV screen and President George W. Bush appeared. Steven Sanders turned up the sound.

"Today, our fellow citizens, our way of life, our very freedom came under attack in a series of deliberate and desperate terrorist acts…The pictures of airplanes flying into buildings, fires burning, huge structures collapsing, have filled us with disbelief, terrible sadness and… unyielding anger…." Kelly clenched her fists.

"Terrorist attacks can shake the foundation of our biggest buildings, but they cannot touch the foundation of America. These acts shatter steel, but they cannot dent the steel of American resolve…Today, our nation saw evil, the very worst of human nature, and we responded with the best of America, with the daring of our rescue workers, with the caring for strangers and neighbors who came to give blood and help in any way they could…."

Kelly was totally engaged. Her parents, conditioned by years in university classrooms, listened to the President with both respect and skepticism. Stephen Sanders squirmed when Bush promised to find those responsible and "bring them to justice. We will make no distinction between the terrorists who committed these acts and those who harbor them…."

Sanders threw up his arms, "Of course, we have to bring justice. But Bush is threatening half the nations in the world. Terrorists live everywhere. He's calling us to war. We can't fight the whole world!"

"We have to fight, Dad!" Kelly yelled.

Her passions boiled over. She didn't agree with her father's 1970's era pacifist views.

"They've killed thousands, Dad. You knew some of them. My friend Molly's folks are probably buried in that rubble. They were innocent and didn't deserve to die!"

Her mother gave him the zip-the-lip look and said, "Kelly, we don't know for sure that Molly's parents have been killed."

"Those who died were someone's friends or someone's family," Kelly retorted. "We have to defend ourselves!"

The President's TV voice agreed with Kelly, "America and our friends and allies…stand together to win the war against terrorism…."

Stephen Sanders muttered, "At what cost?"

The President concluded "None of us will ever forget this day, yet we go forward to defend freedom and all that is good and just in our world. Thank you. Good night and God bless America."

Kelly wondered if God had cursed America. They watched people flee from the poisoned Big Apple. The Sanders family stopped talking and searched for Molly Garvin's parents' faces in the panic-stricken crowds fleeing to the Brooklyn Bridge.

CHAPTER TWENTY-ONE:
Assembly

Wednesday, September 12, 2001

The next day, Kelly Sanders joined the throng of students filing into the West Branch High School auditorium. Counselor Marilyn Kerr had convinced her principal to call an all-school assembly to allow students to express feelings and receive reassurance. "You're in charge," he told her. She lined up students and teachers to speak. At 1:55pm, she led the principal, two teachers, four students and two local pastors onto the stage. The crowd stood reverently when two Boy Scouts carried in the colors. American flags were springing up all over West Branch. Shock and fear revealed old patriotism and a new unity.

Mrs. Kerr stepped to the podium, "We've been through a lot since yesterday morning. There's much we can't understand or don't know yet, but we know we need to pull together. That's why we're here today." She asked one of the pastors to offer a prayer.

"I invite you to pray for the thousands of victims and their families...for the first responders...for our country's leaders...and for our enemies." The room rustled with an unspoken disagreement, 'Why should we pray for our enemies?' But when the pastor said,

"Let us pray," the students hushed. A few sobs punctuated what must have been the longest silence in school history. Marilyn bowed and prayed for the students who had confided in her. The preacher's amen startled her. The principal said a few words and introduced the first student speaker.

Senior class president John Armstrong said, "It was very devastating to realize I was watching thousands of innocent people die. It taught me what is important in life."

Judy Smothers was next, "Talking about it yesterday helped. Last night I just went home, turned off the TV and listened to music. I cried a lot too."

"I think it is very tragic, but we are doing what needs to be done and are all trying to cope as a society," government teacher Robert Urberger said,

Junior Larry Hoffman said, "I want to thank the school administration for cancelling classes yesterday so we could watch the attack together. It was horrible to experience, but the whole world needed to see what happened."

Marilyn felt the crowd stir as a senior on the front row stood, hesitated, then walked to the stage and asked to speak. "I was worried and scared for my new friend Kelly who has friends near the World Trade Center. She doesn't know yet if they are dead or alive. I don't know how I could have handled that...." She hurried down the steps and hugged Kelly Sanders who sat next to Paul Lovejoy. Lovejoy was jolted by what the next speaker said.

"When my mother passed away, I cried forever. Life will never be the same!" Mary Belle Reynolds sat down quickly, looked at her feet and wiped away tears. Counselor Kerr tried to make eye contact with Paul Lovejoy, but couldn't. His posture mimicked the last speaker.

English teacher Margaret Taylor went to the podium. "Yesterday's events have been called, 'horrific', 'barbaric', 'evil.' Those of you in my senior English classes have been reading J.R.R. Tolkien's *The Fellowship of the Ring* about a nice little hobbit who is called to save the world from evil. We have experienced the 'spreading evil' that Tolkien wrote about fifty years ago."

Government teacher Urberger spoke again. "I don't think President Bush ever attended one of Ms. Taylor's English classes, but he agrees with her. Last night, Bush said, 'This enemy hides in the shadows and has no regard for human life.' We are no longer America, land of the safe and secure; we are America, the vulnerable. Tragedies like this can happen anytime or anywhere."

A junior, in a letter jacket, bolted up the stairs and took the mike, "I think about those who died or were injured and I'm glad that none of this happened to me or my family. That sucks." Marilyn tried to listen carefully to each speaker, but couldn't escape her role as time keeper. She asked her pastor to close with a few words of encouragement. He seldom turned down an opportunity to speak. She introduced him.

He leaned into the microphone, "These have been hard days. You're probably still in shock and are trying to process this. I know I am. I wonder what will happen next. What can we do? We always have choices. Horrible things like this can drive us to despair, hate or bitterness. Or we can let them drive us to God and to each other. On the cross Jesus cried out, 'My God, my God, why have you forsaken me.' Evil and death seemed to win. But they didn't. Goodness and life won. Jesus rose. Evil lost. The evils of 9/11 will not win. Don't forget Romans 8:28, 'We know that all things work together for good for those who love God...' Don't give up on God or on life!"

CHAPTER TWENTY-TWO:
Axed

Thursday, September 13, 2001

"We can't give up, yet," the U of I Parkinson's Research team leader blurted out. They were anxiously waiting to meet with new department head Dr. Ruth Sanders. What happened in New York, D.C. and Pennsylvania two days ago didn't change things for them. The wheels of academia ground on. The Lab Rats hoped September 13th would not be their unluckiest day. The three men and two women clustered at one end of the oval conference table, fearing the power of the one who would walk through the door. Sander's reputation as a no-nonsense cost-cutter got to Iowa before she left New York. Programs would be eliminated, projects terminated. Dr. Sanders was no slouch as a researcher but had made her mark in administrative leanness.

A grim Dr. Ruth Sanders entered the room, introduced herself and apologized for the timing of the meeting, "I've lost close friends in New York's terrorist attack, but life has to go on." She gathered herself together, opened her briefcase and pulled out a stack of papers. Sanders gave them each copies. "Our department is about research and teaching. Research like yours is essential to the

University's mission and effectiveness. Clostridium Botulinum may someday prove effective as a treatment for Parkinson's...." They felt the axe coming. "But I have reviewed your research data from the last two years and although it is imaginative, it is inconclusive. Your project is costly and no results are in sight. These defects push your research to the bottom of our department's priority list. I'm sorry that budgets are so tight right now. We'll continue to seek funding for the second phase of the study, but that seems unlikely. Your research grant funds will end on December 31."

The Lab Rat five couldn't look at each other.

"We are beyond the deadline and have been unable to construct a funding plan for Phase II." She saw the mixture of disappointment, frustration and anger. "We will do our best to help you find new lines of research or facilitate your joining one of the other funded projects. The University of Iowa values you and will support your continued academic progress."

CHAPTER TWENTY-THREE:
Anger

Friday, September 14, 2001

Ascruffy student sat alone in the back booth, creating a classic
Norman Rockwell portrait of isolation. He was ignored by the
waitress at Iowa City's *Joint*. She kept wiping sleep from her eyes as
she wearily thumbed through a magazine. The customer picked at his
scrambled eggs, eyes glued on the T.V. He watched the 9/11 news
reports for the thousandth time. America's growing anger at 9/11
fueled his personal anger. The Washington politico spin doctors
made him sick. Politicians and budget slashing university politicians
enraged him. His life had been ruined and he felt like throwing his
cold eggs at the TV. 'If I'd been given a remote with my coffee, I'd
shut them all down.' His anger welded him to the blurry images of
terrorist violence - planes crashing into towers, towers crumbling,
plumes of smoke and death.

His attention was captured by a left-wing commentator, "How
do you like it America? You want to dish out military violence
around the world, but don't want it in your city!" Don't blame Iraq,
Afghanistan or Saudi Arabia. We need to look in the mirror. It's our
own fault. We had it coming. Pillage the world's resources and the

world will make you pay. 9/11 was pay day. Why should we be surprised? Our right-wingers have long warned that we will reap what we have sown. For once the right was right! Why should we be surprised that crowds around the world applauded and danced in the streets? We had it coming. What if Iraq or Iran did this? Why shouldn't they? Americans care nothing except for their oil and the money to be made. No wonder the Arab world hates us! They see us for the materialistic hypocrites we are! Watch out 'Ugly America,' this is just the beginning."

The lone listener hammered the table sending his coffee cup crashing to the floor, "America had it coming. Someone had to pay!" The startled waitress dropped her magazine, but couldn't understand the mumbling from the back booth, "If I had a plane to crash into Iowa's academic towers, I'd make them pay!"

When she went to his booth to sweep up the broken cup, he said, "I'd like a glass of milk."

A strange smile spread across his face as he drank it.

CHAPTER TWENTY-FOUR:
Rubble

Saturday, September 15, 2001

Dr. Ruth Sanders stepped across the family Great Room and shut off the TV. "I can't stand any more of this. We still don't know...."

"We know that Molly's folks are dead!" her daughter contradicted.

"Honey, they're presumed dead, lost somewhere in the rubble."

Kelly snapped, "I don't know whether to cry or scream! Nothing makes any difference – test scores, scholarships, colleges, careers. Nothing means anything now!" She threw the remote across the room.

"We aren't helpless, Kelly. Your dad and I have talked about going back to New York to help our old colleagues test the water and air for toxins. We're trying to get it arranged."

"Will you visit Marie?" Kelly asked.

"If we can; but air travel to New York is still messed up. I'm so relieved Marie emailed us to let us know she's OK." Ruth sighed.

Kelly said, "I'd rather hear her voice on the phone." Just then, the phone rang. Ruth grabbed it. Both hoped it was Marie. It wasn't.

Ruth gripped the phone and her face got redder and redder. Kelly couldn't tell anything about the phone call except that it was upsetting her mother.

"Go ahead and make your appeal to the Dean!" Ruth said as she slammed down the phone.

"Who was that?" Kelly asked.

"A student who is very angry with me," she said.

"Why? What did you do?"

"We had to terminate his doctoral project. His research study was creative, but results just weren't there," Ruth answered.

"What will happen?"

"The project will be terminated at the end of the year. No grants, no research funding. Some very bright students will see their academic world go down the drain."

"Why should they be spared?" Kelly exclaimed, "Everything is being terminated - New York, our security and our freedom. Terrorists have ruined our lives! You and dad can go back and help in the Big Apple. I can't do anything."

Ruth tried to comfort her daughter but got a cold shoulder instead of a hug.

CHAPTER TWENTY-FIVE:
Connection

Tuesday, September 18, 2001

Chaplain Herb Lovejoy trudged along the first floor hallway at University Hospital. It was a grim Tuesday morning, one week after the 9/11 terrorist attacks. Monday's stock market dropped a record 684 points. Herb found no comfort in how little the market's drop affected his meager investments. He could identify with the victims; he knew how much personal capital he'd lost in September 1999.

Walking beside him, Chaplain Connie Baughman broke into his reflections, "Herb, are you all right?" They were heading out to do their rounds.

"I'm sorry, Connie. This last week has taken me to a dark place... I know we are supposed to be bearers of light."

She sensed something surfacing. "Have time for coffee this afternoon?"

"Sounds good," He said. "...Would you to do me favor? I know you're assigned to Neonatal ICU today. Would you check in on Billy Griffin; he's almost two-weeks-old. I haven't been able to see him this week." She agreed. His pager beeped. An oncology nurse pleaded for a chaplain. Herb took elevator E to the cancer floor and the nurse pointed him to the room.

"Robert Simmons is terminal and death is imminent. His family could use some support. We've done all we can medically." Spiritual care was often called in when medical care ran out of options. He knocked gently on the door to 4469. A family member welcomed him.

Diane Simmons lay on the bed beside her dying husband. She held his left hand which wasn't hooked up to the morphine drip. Mrs. Simmons paid no attention to Herb but talked to her dying husband as she squeezed his hand, "Bob, it's OK to let go. You've been so brave, so very brave. You fought the Big C as long as you could...Don't worry about me, honey. The boys will take care of me, I'll be OK." His hand slipped from hers and she grabbed it again.

The eldest son, who had been taking his dad's pulse, said, "He's gone, Mom." The younger son took her by the shoulders and pulled her away.

"I don't want to leave him," she cried. "Bob, Bob, honey, I love you." Her sons hugged her and held her. It was a sacred moment.

Tears streaming down her face, Simmons sobbed, "Chaplain, this is the most horrible day of my life...." He didn't tell her about his most horrible day.

Two hours later, he carried a fresh cup of coffee into Chaplain Connie Baughman's office and sat in her spare chair. She said, "Little Billy in NICU is making good progress; his mother got to hold him today for the first time!" He thanked her and they chatted for a moment. She pointed to the picture frame behind her desk, "Herb, what do you think of my motto, 'Keep your ears open and your mouth shut.'?"

"Not always easy to do, is it?" he replied

"No. but listening is important." She leaned forward and her eyes locked on to his. "That's why I invited you up for coffee. I wanted to offer you a listening ear." She had his full attention. "Herb, you are a good listener, but how good are you at talking?" He looked uncertain. "You seem troubled by something. I didn't know if it was 9/11, the work here, or something personal. I don't mean to pry...."

"Connie, your antennae is working way too well," he answered. "It's personal...." Herb looked away, collected himself and blurted out, "I'm still grieving Brenda and Sarah's deaths- my wife and daughter. I've kept it all bottled up."

"Go ahead and pour some of it out," Connie said, encouraging him to continue talking, "I haven't lost a spouse to death but I have lost one to divorce," she added. "Divorce is a kind of death and has its own grief too. Dreams and plans are buried. Talking helps the healing come."

Herb said, "I hope so."

"What was your wife like?" she asked.

Herb hesitated to answer, struck again by how much she reminded him of Brenda. "Sorry. I had a passing thought. Brenda was my tower of strength for fifteen years. Her faith nudged me along. She supported me when I felt called into the ministry. She worked to provide for us, while I took my three-year journey through seminary...."

"Knowing the demands of seminary, I'd bet she was almost a single mom." Connie said.

"She was. Brenda was a remarkable mom." Herb wished he could be as good a dad. "She was also a great wife, who laughed at my jokes, critiqued my sermons and covered up my mistakes."

"Sounds like a wonderful person. I wish I could have met her."

"You remind me of her," Herb said.

"I'll take that as a compliment." He thought she blushed. They weren't sure what else to say. Their professional conversation had taken a personal turn. Her beeping pager rescued them.

CHAPTER TWENTY-SIX:
Heavenbound

Thursday, September 20, 2001

Two days later, the nation was still reeling from the staggering blows of 9/11. Herb Lovejoy drove home from the University Hospital thinking about how death had toppled his personal twin towers of wife Brenda and daughter Sarah. Like everyone else, Herb wanted life to get back to normal. But he knew the new normal meant he was still a widower and America was still in crisis. 'I've got to get it together and be there for Paul,' he thought before finding a gap in the traffic and pulling off I-80. Paul's new school friend Kelly was coming over to study. Herb knew she was from New York City and could only imagine what she was going through.

Her car was already in the driveway, so Herb parked in the soggy grass under the gnarled maple tree. The two seniors were sitting together in the kitchen. An empty pizza box, books and papers were scattered over the table. The TV droned in the background with 9/11 stories - firefighter and police heroes, survivors, and speculations about U.S. military responses. Herb greeted Paul and Kelly, made small talk, and retreated to the living room.

He heard her anger from his recliner. "New York, my home, was attacked. Paul, I just don't understand it!" Her feelings were raw. "Where was God in all of this?" Mentioning God ignited a series of questions that led her to ask, "Preacher boy, I've got a question - do dogs get into Heaven?"

Paul said, "Dad. Dad! I need help in here."

Herb feared that he was going to be grilled again about 9/11 and God's will. He was relieved when Kelly just asked about God and animals. "Mr. Lovejoy, do dogs go to heaven?" She was dead serious. "Nobody has ever told me how God fits in with animals; except for one smart-aleck who said, "G-o-d is d-o-g spelled backwards."

"I wouldn't put it that way," Herb answered. "Actually animals are important in the bible."

"Really?" she said.

"Let me show you." He pulled his bible off the kitchen shelf, where it was sandwiched between two unused cook books. I just thought you might want to read what it says for yourself."

"OK, show me," she responded.

Herb sat in the chair Paul had vacated, pushed the pizza box aside and opened the bible to the Genesis creation story. "Read it right here on the first page, chapter one, verses 24-25."

"I don't get that chapter-verse lingo."

"The numbers help us find stuff," he answered. "See the 24? Start reading there."

"And God said, 'Let the earth bring forth living creatures of every kind: cattle and creeping things and wild animals of the earth of every kind.'" Herb searched his pastoral memory for his best answer to the dog-and-heaven question. Kelly finished, "It says that 'God saw that it was good.' So, God thinks animals are good?"

"Absolutely! That's why God made so many of them. The bible has animal stories all the way through."

"Like what?" she asked.

"There's a funny one about a talking donkey."

"I don't believe you." For a moment she forgot 9/11.

He flipped through pages until he found Numbers 22. "Here it is. A man named Balaam was riding his donkey through a narrow passageway. God spoke to Balaam and told him to stop. He wouldn't listen, but his donkey heard God and lay right down on the path. When Balaam beat the donkey, God spoke through the donkey to Balaam."

"So the donkey understood what God said?" When Herb nodded, Kelly exclaimed, "I've always believed animals understand what we say. Are dogs ever mentioned?"

Herb hesitated. "There's an Old Testament proverb warning that to repeat mistakes is to be like a dog returning to eat its own vomit."

"Gross! What's that about?"

"We should avoid repeating our mistakes," he explained.

"I get that."

Herb continued, "Another story tells how a woman asked Jesus for help. He refused her. She told him, 'Look at the dogs under the table, they at least get the scraps from the table. Am I less than a dog?' Jesus helped her."

"Women and dogs deserve more than scraps!" she exclaimed.

"You really like dogs don't you?"

"I love them. My dog Darth saved my life and loves me unconditionally. I can't say that for people," she admitted.

Herb said, "Yesterday a hospital therapist told us how dogs can help in the healing process, 'There's no psychiatrist in the world like a puppy licking your face.' Jesus talked about that."

"He did?"

"Yes. He told a story about a rich guy named Lazarus who suffered for taking advantage of poor people. He was comforted when dogs licked his wounds."

"Dogs love us," Kelly agreed. "I just don't understand why we're so mean to animals? I had a neighbor boy who bragged about torturing a stray cat. I saw a TV show about the abuse of wild horses. Last week, on our fieldtrip, I saw how a farmer locks up his cattle.

Farm jails! Animals have rights too! We're cruel. Why do we think we're better than they are? Only human beings are terrorists!" 9/11 reared its ugly head. Herb held his tongue. She was getting riled up. "Reverend Lovejoy, you still didn't answer my question about whether dogs go to heaven. If dogs don't go to Heaven I don't want to go there!" She took a breath. "Anyhow, how does God decide who gets to Heaven and who doesn't? And why did all those people in New York have to die?" He started to respond. But she glanced at the clock and cut him off, "Sorry, I've got to get home! My folks are flying to New York City tomorrow. They're going to help analyze the toxins at Ground Zero." She gathered up her books and bolted into the living room for a last word to Paul, "I know I told you I was going to become a veterinarian and save animals. But I don't want to wait five years. I just figured out something I can do right now!"

When she left, Herb said, "Whew! Why did you ever tell her I was a preacher?"

"You were, weren't you?"

"But, Paul, I'm not exactly one now."

"Don't you do God's work at the hospital?" his son asked.

"I don't know, but it's not the same as preaching in a church."

"Isn't University Hospital your church now?"

"Paul, this ex-preacher, wanna-be-chaplain is talked out. I need some shut-eye," Herb sighed.

"Dad, when you're not so tired, I'd like your take on 9/11; and maybe you can answer Kelly's question about who gets into Heaven."

CHAPTER TWENTY-SEVEN:
Protest

Saturday, September 22, 2001

It was a tough Saturday for farmer Jerry Kerr - milking the cows, moving six calves, replacing a mower blade and dealing with three salesmen. To top it off, his wife Marilyn was off grocery shopping in Iowa City. He was moving a load of hay when three cars, a van and a pickup truck skidded into his gravel driveway and blocked him in. A dozen teenagers jumped out waving placards and chanting, 'Free the Cows.' Other signs waved, 'SOAR—Society of Animal Rights'. It was a full-blown protest led by the perky blonde from last week's dairy tour. Marilyn had teased him when he talked about noticing the girl. "You always have an eye for the pretty ones."

But the protest-girl wasn't so cute with her angry face and her ridiculous slogans. Jerry was getting mad. He had work to do. Their chants and placards rekindled both 911 and Nam. He got off his green machine, remembering how it felt to get off the plane in Chicago back in1965. Like many Vietnam War Veterans, he was welcomed home by angry protesters waving signs and shouting slogans. Old feelings of disgust boiled to the surface.

"What do you kids know about animals?" Jerry shouted.

Someone yelled back, "We know not to confine them. They have a life too!"

"They do," the farmer said. "Thanks to me, they're fed and watered. How many cows have you fed this week?"

"Animal abuser! Confiner! Jailer! Killer!" the little bombshell shouted.

Bombshells exploded in Jerry Kerr's head. It was no longer 2001. He was teleported back to December 1965. Corporal J.F. Kerr's unit had survived one of the most devastating battles of the war. Shrapnel tore his right thigh, but he lived through it. Half his unit was killed or shipped to hospitals in Japan. His unit landed in Chicago to be mustered out. When the soldiers stepped off the plane, they were attacked by shouting anti-war protesters. He remembered how his buddy-for-life, Mike Davis, stiffened when the peaceniks smacked him across the face with a 'Make Peace, Not War' sign. Mike didn't break stride, but said through clenched teeth, "I'd rather run through elephant grass than walk through these grass-smoking hippies." The soldiers continued through the terminal without flinching or acknowledging the protesters. "We fought for America's freedom, and this is the thanks we get!"

But 7th Cavalry Corporal Jerry Franklin Kerr was going to fight back this time. He pounded his fists against the tractor tire. "Get off my property! Move your cars."

"We're not moving until the cows are freed!" they chanted back.

Kerr didn't back down. This was not Chicago in '65, but West Branch in 2001. He shook his fist, "I'm calling the police on you!"

Kerr stomped to the house, called Chief Curtis and got himself a beer. 'I need to calm down.'

Kelly Saunders couldn't calm down. She was pumped by 9/11, the confrontation and her crusade. When West Branch's Police Chief booted them off the farm, she called him 'Barney Fife.' The rebuffed protesters avoided the police station on their way back to West Branch's only teen hangout. They were amped from the confrontation. Some came for the thrill; four of the girls were true animal lovers; two were Kelly's new friends; and six guys who didn't particularly care for cows, but liked the girls who did. Paul was one of them.

As the teens jockeyed for tables, Paul found a place beside Kelly. He knew her folks were back in New York City helping at Ground Zero. Kelly was left behind to wage her personal war against animal abuse and to deal with her feelings about the attack on her city. "Kelly, could we grab a bite to eat in Iowa City, take in a movie or something?" Paul asked.

She shrugged, "OK. Right now, anything sounds better than West Branch. I'll drive my car home and take care of Darth. Pick me up there in an hour? Thanks, Paul. I need to talk; my thinker is exploding."

Paul considered it a first date. Kelly talked his head off in the restaurant. She was exhilarating and a bit overwhelming. Being with Kelly charged Paul's batteries. She was glad for a guy who really listened to her. She talked a mile a minute and neither paid much attention to the food. When they walked back to the car she took his hand. It felt good. He left a casual girlfriend back in Joliet and figured Kelly left a bunch of broken-hearts in New York. Paul opened the door for her, remembering what his mother had said about treating girls with respect.

Kelly said, "Thank you sir" and slid as close to him as the bucket seat would allow. She talked all the way home. Paul pulled into her driveway and turned off the car motor. She said, "Better turn off the lights too." They talked more. She touched his left cheekbone. "Where did you get that scar?"

The tables were turned. He talked, telling her about losing his mother and sister. Impulsively, she kissed his scar. He kissed her back on her cheek. She kissed him on the mouth then punched his right arm. "Don't worry, silly, you're not the first....my dog Darth and I kiss all the time." Paul kissed her again.

She kissed him back. She was enjoying this and so was he. Passions rose. Kelly thought, 'Don't let this go too far, too fast.' She remembered her friend back in New York who got pregnant at 16. Theresa's career dreams were flushed down the drain by one night of passion and an unplanned pregnancy. 'I don't want that to happen to me.' Kelly gently pushed Paul away. "Would you walk me to the door, Mr. Lovejoy?" She lightened the mood, "Or is it 'Loverboy'?" Not wanting to reignite the fire, she gave him a quick good night kiss and unlocked the front door.

CHAPTER TWENTY-EIGHT:
Poisoned

Wednesday, September 26, 2001

The doorbell rang. "Who could that be?" Jerry Kerr mumbled to his wife. The blurry clock radio said 3:00 am.

Marilyn said, "Put on your pants and see who it is! I can't stand that infernal door bell."

"I got that bell on sale at Wal-Mart."

She poked him and he climbed out of bed. She thought he still moved pretty well for someone almost 60. Jerry thought, 'Damn, I feel old!' He pulled on his pants and groped to the kitchen door and jerked it open. He was met with an apology.

"Sorry to wake you, Mr. Kerr."

"Marvin, what's the problem?" In the fifteen years Marvin had been picking up his milk and hauling it to Iowa City, this was only the second time he'd awakened Jerry. Marvin hoped there wouldn't be a third time.

The truck driver gestured toward the barns, "Something's wrong in your milk tank room. I saw someone dart out when I pulled in. I went inside and the cap on the milk tank was askew. Then I saw it...."

"Saw what?"

"A broken flask," the driver said.

"What kind of flask?" Jerry asked.

"Like one from a high school chemistry lab."

"So it was a break in!" Pulling his jacket over his t-shirt, he said, "Let's take a look."

"I've got a flashlight," Marvin said.

"Don't worry! I know the way in the dark. What did the intruder look like? Did you see him?"

Struggling to keep pace with the agitated farmer, Marvin answered, "No. I never got a look at the face…didn't seem very tall…but ran scared, like a chipmunk chased by a dog." They walked through the wash of truck lights into the milk house.

Kerr saw the open tank lid and the broken bottle, "Did they contaminate my milk? Who knows what they might have dumped into it? You can't pump it, Marvin. I'm calling the police chief." Shaking his head, he added, "In thirty years, I'd never called cops to come out here until last week when I needed him to take care of those crazy kids."

"Kids?"

"High school animal rights kids blocked my driveway and accused me of cow abuse."

"You think one of them…."

"Who knows?" He thought of the angry blonde who led the protest. "Anyway, as they say on the new C.S.I. detective show, 'This is now a crime scene.' I'm calling the West Branch police chief!"

"So early?" Marvin asked.

"You bet. Phil Curtis is a buddy from high school. I have to get my milk tank emptied so I can milk my cows; they can't wait, their udders will explode." Kerr continued to lecture the driver while the phone rang, "A dairy cow is genetically bred to overproduce milk and if you don't milk her regularly, milk flow slows down and won't recover until she has her next calf…."

The Chief's sleepy voice interrupted, "Chief Curtis. Who is this?"

"Jerry Kerr. Sorry to wake you Phil, but I've got an emergency!"

"What's wrong? Your teenage friends burn down your barns?"

"No. but it looks like someone has poisoned my milk."

That got the chief's attention. Half an hour later, the police cruiser bounced up the driveway and parked next to the milk truck. After hearing the driver's story, the chief quickly surveyed the scene, "I've got to go back to my car and get my stuff." Curtis returned with his camera and an assortment of evidence bags.

"The broken bottle is over here," the truck driver said as he reached for it.

"Don't touch that! I need to secure the scene, take fingerprints and collect evidence before we touch anything."

"So you're a C.S.I.?" the driver asked.

"Don't I wish! But I know enough to use gloves when I bag evidence. Let's do it." Curtis took photographs of the broken flask and the milk tank. Then he took another set of photos with a ruler laid beside the broken flask and the open lidded stainless steel tank. Jerry Kerr wanted to hurry things along.

"Easy Jerry, I know you need to milk your precious cows soon. We have to do this by the book. It looks like the milk in your tank has been compromised. It's beyond suspicious. You'll have to dump it, but not before I take samples for testing."

"Will you use yellow tape to mark the crime scene?" Marvin asked.

"Leave the police work to me. I wouldn't tell you how to drive your truck. Just don't touch anything...and come to think of it, don't walk outside. There may be footprints."

Kerr pleaded, "Come on Phil, I want to get this guy as much as you do. But I have 85 cows I need to milk in an hour. They'll shut down if I don't milk them soon. I'm already losing one tank of milk. I can't afford to lose more."

"I understand, Jerry. But you need to understand that I have to take samples of milk to send to DCI lab in Des Moines. After photographing that broken flask, I'm going to dust it for prints. I'll dust the top of the tank, your milk stopper and your doorknob. I'll photograph any footprint impressions outside." The policeman opened his notebook, "Marvin, tell me again what you saw this morning." The driver described the short, fleeing figure whose face was hidden by a black-hooded sweat shirt.

Marvin asked, "Could this guy have been a terrorist, like 9/11?"

"Time will tell. Jerry, any strangers visit the farm lately?"

Kerr answered, "We had fifty or sixty people here for our big tour two weeks ago, mostly neighbors and students. Phil, you already met our most suspicious visitors. You ran them off last Saturday."

"I haven't forgotten, Jerry. Do you have any of their names?"

"I don't know the ringleader's name, but she's one of my wife's new kids. Talk to Marilyn before you start your manhunt."

"OK, I'll ask her. By the way, we don't call them 'manhunts' anymore. It's not politically correct and the perp might be female. I'll talk to Marilyn before I leave. When I finish, I need to call State DCI and notify the County Sheriff in Tipton." Curtis wrapped up his work and asked Marvin for his phone number, "I'll need an official statement from you later." He told Jerry, "I've got my samples, so you can dump that milk down the drain. Use extra disinfectant on the inside of the tank but don't touch the outside surfaces. The big boys may want to double-check my work. They aren't sure we local yokels know what we're doing. Use rubber gloves here in the milk room, the experts may be able to find prints I missed." He waved on his way out, "I'll refrigerate these milk samples and get them to state lab a.s.a.p."

Jerry Kerr turned the tank spigot and watched the white river of milk gush down the drain. "There go my profits for September. No insurance protection for me. I'm just a farmer; I didn't build a fancy house on a floodplain next to a river that floods every year." The flood of milk slowed to a trickle, then a drip. Kerr hosed down the last bubbles.

Chief Curtis finished questioning Marilyn before Jerry had cleaned the contaminated tank.

CHAPTER TWENTY-NINE:
Arrest

Wednesday, September 26, 2001

Darth barked and Kelly Sanders jumped up from the table. She grabbed her favorite black sweatshirt from the hallway closet and pulled it on. 'How can the bus be here already?' She was surprised to see a police cruiser pulling into the driveway. Two uniforms got out. 'Why are they here? Did something happen to Mom and Dad?' Kelly opened the door just as Chief Curtis was ready to knock. She recognized him. He was the one she called 'Barney Fife' when he chased her SOAR group off the farm. "Officer, what do you want?"

With a wary eye on the big dog, Curtis stepped inside, followed by a deputy. He stared at her sweatshirt, then said, "Miss Sanders, we're investigating an act of vandalism or possible terrorism. Where were you at 3:00 this morning?"

"What kind of a question is that? I was right here, home alone in bed. My parents are helping at Ground Zero in New York. My friends were killed by terrorists. I'm no terrorist! I'm eighteen, old enough to be here alone. And none of this is any of your damned business!"

Darth growled when she raised her voice.

"Miss, watch your tongue and restrain your dog! I'm not afraid to shoot him."

"You stay the hell away from him!" She stepped into the chief's face.

In a split second the dog lunged, the deputy jerked backwards and Kelly took a swing at Chief Curtis. Her unlucky-lucky jab to his chin caught him off guard and decked him.

The next thing she knew she was face-down on the floor gasping for breath and wearing hand cuffs. The knee in the middle of her back took the fight out of her.

"Young lady, you are under arrest for assaulting a police officer. You have the right to...."

"I know my rights," she grunted back. "I just want to know what's going on. Why is this happening?" The chief read Kelly the rest of her Miranda rights without answering her question. He wiped blood from his mouth with one hand and pulled her up with the other. The deputy held the angry dog at bay with a kitchen chair. For a split second, he envisioned himself in a circus, holding back a vicious lion. He was brought back to reality by his boss's voice.

"We're all going to Tipton to get some answers." Curtis told his deputy, "This criminal and I are going out the front door to the county jail. Lock that Labrador mutt in the house before you follow us out." He hustled her down the front steps.

'Why do handcuffs make me walk funny?' Kelly wondered. She hoped the school bus would not come by. Halfway to the squad car, she realized how much trouble she was in, "I'm sorry. I'm sorry. I didn't mean to do it."

CHAPTER THIRTY:
Crisis

Thursday, September 27, 2001

Chaplain Herb Lovejoy waited impatiently for the elevator. When the door finally opened, he stepped aside to let a nurse push a wheelchair out into the hallway. The kid in the chair looked about Paul's age. Two doctors got on the elevator with him, engrossed in conversation, "I don't understand the spike in pulmonary admissions?"

"And why are so many of them college kids?" the other one said.

The taller doctor shrugged, "We're usually treating an older demographic. I may find out more this afternoon. The higher-ups have called a special interdepartmental meeting. Something's going on. I'll let you know...."

Herb left them in the elevator and made his last visits before lunch. He threaded his way through hallway traffic, and waved to an Emergency Treatment Center (ETC) admission's supervisor whose desk faced the hallway. Herb knew her from his first week in Iowa City. She beckoned him over.

"What's up, Sally?" he asked.

"Chaplain, can I bend your ear for a minute?"

"Sure," Herb replied and stepped closer to her desk.

"I'm not sure it's anything," she said, "but I found an anomaly in our registration profiles today. Statistically, it's strange. Like an improbable probability."

"Probability?" he raised an eyebrow.

Sally said. "Pardon the lingo. I started out as a statistic's major but ended up here. Life's journeys are never predictable, are they?"

"You got that! What's out of sync?"

She turned her computer screen so he could see it. "Forty percent of our new admits are U of I students...."

"It is a university town," Herb interjected.

"Yes. But normally, less than ten percent of our new patients are students."

"That low?" he asked.

"The young may not be as invincible as they think, but they are healthier."

Herb remembered the teen in the wheelchair. "Have you talked to anyone up the command chain?"

Sally shrugged, "I've thought about it."

"If you see a pattern, it might be worth passing along."

"You may be right, chaplain... I think I will call it in."

Herb hurried to keep his lunch date with Connie Baughman.

They had taken overlapping paths on their morning rounds. Baughman, touched by 9/11 stories of heroism, was resolved to be more attentive to the hospital's support staff. 'They are ordinary, everyday heroes. A hospital can't run without them.' Her intentional stride took her to Radiology.

A young woman looked up from her computer screen, "Can I help you?"

"Actually, I wanted to thank you for the help you give to our patients," Connie said.

"I don't hear that often. I've seen you around. You're a chaplain, aren't you?"

"I am. How's your day going?"

"A little crazy. We've been hit with a spike in CT scan orders from the ETC Docs."

A chirping phone interrupted them. After the phone call, she turned back to Connie,

"Something's wrong. We keep getting more requests. Sorry, chaplain, but I've got to get these processed."

Connie breathed a silent prayer and headed downstairs to the Emergency Treatment Center. She glanced into the waiting room and saw three tearful young women clustered together. She walked in. "Hi, I'm Chaplain Baughman, anything I can do?"

"Our three best friends and dorm mates were admitted today," the most composed replied. "One has double vision and slurred speech; the other two act like they've had strokes. Doctors are doing a bunch of blood tests, scans and stuff."

Connie thought it seemed strange that three students from the same dorm would have strokes on the same day. She kept her opinion to herself and spoke professionally, "If that's what's wrong, they're in the right place. Can I sit and chat a minute?" It was a fruitful conversation. She affirmed them for contacting all three sets of parents.

One lamented, "But we couldn't get hold of Megan's folks and had to leave a message."

"The six of us are so close!" another explained. "We hang together so much that we're known as 'the six pack'. We feel guilty that we missed breakfast with them yesterday. We were cramming for exams and just slept in."

After another fifteen minutes of conversation, Connie glanced at the wall clock and stood. "Sorry to run, but I've got a lunch date. Stay together and stay strong." She walked into the cafeteria and saw Chaplain Lovejoy at the salad bar.

He greeted her, "Hi Connie. Good day?"

"Yes. I got to spend half-an-hour with three college students." The chaplains slid their trays along the food rails. Herb realized how much he didn't know about her.

After a table prayer, he asked, "What made your time with the students so special?"

"They took me back to the best time of my life," she said. "You know. Living away from home, new friends from all over the country, stimulating classes...."

"Guys?" he asked.

"Of course! I started out majoring in college men."

"How'd you get any studying done?"

She smiled slyly, "Smart dorm mates kept me focused. Guess that's why today was so special...." Herb waited, fork poised. "The three girls in the EMT waiting room were there to support three hospitalized friends. It reminded me of my gal pals back in the day."

"What happened to their three friends?"

"That was weird," Connie said. "The trio came in with similar symptoms: paralysis, speech problems, slurring."

"Strokes?"

"That's what I thought, but it seems unlikely," she said. "The three sick ones ate breakfast together; maybe it was a weird reaction to the food?"

"Dorm food can do that to you," Herb quipped. "Did you say it was the ETC waiting room? We must have just missed each other. I talked with the woman at ETC admissions desk half-an-hour ago. She thought something strange was going on."

The two chaplains weren't the only ones asking questions. A crisis management meeting was convening on the other side of the hospital. University Hospital's best doctors were also asking, "How could so many students come down with the similar symptoms?" Doctors paraded out a circus of possibilities: a flu virus, Lyme disease, bacterial infections, airborne pathogens. Nothing suggested a contagion, but it felt like an epidemic-in-the making. No one wanted to use that e-word. It wasn't an epidemic yet; too early for a definitive diagnosis. Three hours later, rumors of an epidemic spread as more students were admitted. When the Hospital's Chief Medical Officer contacted the University's Health Clinic, Mercy Hospital and local doctors, a growing problem was confirmed.

Down the chain of command, Chaplain Director Elaine Armstrong was informed of the emerging crisis. She implored the chaplains to stay for additional shifts, "In my twenty years, I've never asked a team to do this. Student patients and their families need us, so does the medical staff." Moved by the mounting sense of crisis, they agreed. University of Iowa Hospitals was taking a big hit. It felt like a pandemic: symptoms of Guillain-Barre' syndrome, myasthenia gravis and strokes. Medical laboratory technicians worked 24-7 doing batteries of tests to identify causes, case-by-case. Doctors collaborated to interpret test results and order procedures. The Iowa Department of Public Health was called in; they contacted the Federal Center for Disease Control (CDC). Some doctors feared a bacterial infection or food poisoning. A public health officer, a medical doctor and a University representative went room to room, interviewing students who'd been stricken. The trio discovered a pattern that linked the poisoning to the University of Iowa Food Services. Hillcrest, Burge and Mayflower residence halls were the primary sources. Others had eaten at Memorial Union cafes and delis in the Law and Dental buildings.

The team identified milk as the common food consumed by the afflicted in all locations. Further tests showed that Botulinum was the culprit. Treatment options were challenging. By Friday noon, thirty students were paralyzed, four were on ventilators and ten were in critical condition. It was an unprecedented medical crisis.

Herb tried to help, but felt like he was trying to extinguish a forest fire with a squirt gun. He wanted to go to the chapel and recharge, but had to settle for praying on the run. Parents of a paralyzed student asked, "Chaplain, how in God's name did this happen? How did all these students get sick? Is it an epidemic, mass poisoning, terrorism?"

The story broke in the local media, was picked up by newscasts across Iowa and exploded onto the national stage. Iowa's Department of Public Health tracked the infected milk from University of Iowa dispensing machines back to the dairy processor, Dubuque Street Dairy. Experts determined that the contaminated milk had been processed Tuesday morning, packed for milk machines and delivered to University dorms and cafés that afternoon. The tainted milk was consumed that night and all day Wednesday. Late Friday night, University Food Service tested and dumped all Dubuque Street Dairy milk and cancelled their contract, subject to results of the investigation. The flow of new students being hospitalized slowed, but those already affected got worse. Doctors warned of possible deaths and difficult recoveries. University officials braced for public outrage. Years of positive public relations had been sabotaged.

Chaplain Herb Lovejoy plodded through the hospital food line after working twenty straight hours. He wasn't sure what day it was or what meal he was eating, but he knew he didn't want milk with his meal. He and Chaplain Baughman talked again. Both felt like they'd been on a weekend drinking binge or had just finished finals.

"Why would someone do this?" Connie asked, as she toyed with her food.

Herb didn't have much of an appetite for food either. And he had no answer to her question, so he just shrugged, like a student who hadn't read the assignment.

Connie struggled to put her thoughts into words, "There are a lot of angry, hurting, violent people out there…."

"But, why did they come here and do this?" he asked. Their conversations tapered into an exhausted silence. Both leaned on the wobbly table. Herb's face rested on the back of his hands and sleep called him. His pager ended any thought of sleeping. His son Paul had left an urgent message.

CHAPTER THIRTY-ONE:
Confusion

Friday, September 28, 2001

Herb Lovejoy ran to find a phone. He called Paul at West Branch High School. The office put him on hold. It was a long two minutes until his son spoke.

"Paul, slow down! What happened?" Herb was stunned by his son's answer. "Kelly was accused of what?" Herb listened to the story again. "Paul, I'll get there as soon as I can. Yes, I'll drive you out to Kelly's house. I love you too, son." He hung up, now fully awake.

"What happened?" Connie asked.

"Paul's classmate Kelly Sanders was arrested and jailed for assaulting a police officer. She is also suspected of terrorism. I have to go help them."

Connie breathed another silent prayer as she watched Herb gather his briefcase and raincoat. Twenty minutes later, Herb picked up Paul at West Branch High and they drove northwest to the Sanders' house.

Paul tried to explain, "Kelly punched the police chief when he barged into her house Wednesday morning accusing her of being a terrorist. She thought he was going to hurt her dog. The cops arrested her on the spot and took her to the county jail in Tipton."

"Where are her parents?" Herb asked.

"Remember, she told us they were going to Ground Zero. Kelly couldn't reach them and didn't have anyone else to call. She begged me to take care of Darth."

"Her dog?" Herb's adrenaline was pumping but his mind was still clogged.

"Cops threatened to shoot her dog," Paul said. "He's a big friendly Lab; I can't imagine him attacking anyone!"

"Paul, we can't always predict what dogs or people will do." Paul thought of 9/11. Herb thought about the chaos at the hospital.

"Dad, would you go visit her after you drop me off?"

"Sure." Herb's heart agreed but his body screamed for rest. "Paul, on the phone, I couldn't understand what you meant by milk contamination."

"Something happened at the Kerr dairy farm."

"Where your class toured?" Herb asked.

Paul hung his head. "Yes... I went back to the farm with Kelly and the other protesters...."

"Protesters?" Herb interrupted.

"We were just exercising free speech. We meant no harm. Kelly's such a magnet. A bunch of us followed her back to the Kerr dairy farm on Saturday. We waved a few placards and the cops chased us off. I don't understand how the milk got contaminated. Why would the police go to her house today to arrest her?"

Herb could imagine why. He hoped Paul hadn't been dragged into criminal acts.

Paul continued, "What Kelly told me was unbelievable- she got knocked down, handcuffed and accused of terrorism. I can't figure out what happened, but I know she wants me to take care of her dog. Maybe she can explain everything when you talk to her."

"OK," Herb said. "We're almost to her house. How will you get in? Do you have a key?"

"No, but she told me the combination to the door. It was her grandma's birthday, 11-10-26. Herb watched Paul punch in the code and open the door before he backed down the driveway and drove east toward Tipton.

CHAPTER THIRTY-TWO:
Vandal

The lonely figure huddled on the narrow bed couldn't sleep and shifted to avoid the light through the narrow window. 'I'm a prisoner. What did I expect? The truck headlights blinded me up on top of that steel milk tank. I stumbled down the ladder and dropped the flask of my special brew. It shattered on the concrete floor. Good thing I used latex gloves. Wearing my hooded sweatshirt was a stroke of genius; the truck driver couldn't see my face. I had to flee for my life!'

The culprit had to race through a field of corn, over a fence, into a ditch and through the woods that bordered the road. 'I thought I'd never get to my car.' The carefully planned attack had been executed just like the night before. Everything was the same, except for almost getting caught. The memory was vivid. 'When I got into the car, I closed my door so quietly that even the night crickets in the ditch couldn't hear me. Driving without headlights for five minutes was tricky.' Twice, the vehicle almost slid into the grader ditch. My practice runs helped, but weeds and brush overgrew the narrow dirt road and made driving difficult. 'I know how to drive in the city, but these muddy hillbilly roads are treacherous. Monday night I gave that milk tank a big dose of toxin and no one even knew I'd even been there. Not tonight! I'd cased the farm for watch-dogs, cameras and locks, but never expected the truck!'

CHAPTER THIRTY-THREE:
Jail Confession

Friday, September 28, 2001

Tipton was a small town and Herb had no trouble finding the county jail on the south side of town. The Cedar County Sheriff's Office and Jail was a new building. Herb walked into the lobby which smelled of fresh paint, not the usual jail stench of sweat and cigarette smoke. He told the desk officer, "I want to visit Kelly Sanders."

"Could I see some ID?" He showed her his hospital chaplain's card. "Seems legit, but we require a photo ID." Herb took his Illinois driver's license out of his billfold. She carefully compared the license with the card. She shrugged, "OK," and took him through a metal door into the visitation room which was identified by a cardboard sign held up with masking tape. "Our permanent signs haven't come yet," the officer explained.

Five minutes later, the officer led Kelly Sanders in and sat her down in a chair across from Herb. She couldn't look him in the eye. Instead, she silently stared at her hands clenched on the table. Suddenly, she threw her hands in the air and blurted, "Why is this happening to me, Mr. Lovejoy?" She exploded with anger and frustration, belting out a stream of hard questions. "Why am I sitting here where I don't belong? I haven't done anything. If your God is so loving, why are such horrible things allowed to happen? I didn't do anything but try to protect Darth. You told me God cares for animals. Where is your God?"

Herb fumbled for answers. He had his own questions: Where is God in 9/11? University students paralyzed? Drive-by-shootings? Cancer? Bigotry? Poverty? War? Car wrecks? He couldn't think of anything to say, so they sat in silence. They forged a strange emotional bond.

Kelly broke the silence, "I know you've been through a lot too, Mr. Lovejoy. Paul told me about the car accident back in Illinois. But you can't understand what I'm going through. You've never done anything this bad...."

"You're wrong, Kelly. I killed my wife."

CHAPTER THIRTY-FOUR:
Paper

Friday, September 28, 2001

At dawn, he dropped into an exhausted sleep and dreamed of being chased by cops with bright lights and baying dogs. A thump on the door snapped his eyes open. 'They've come for me!' Hiding behind the curtain, he peeked through the window. The paper boy was pedaling down the sidewalk. It was just the afternoon paper. He cracked open the door and grabbed his paper.

The Press Citizen's banner headline 'Hospital Crisis' electrified him. He devoured the article.

"University of Iowa and Mercy Hospitals treated hundreds of students on Friday. Seven U of I students were in ICU, three in critical condition. 'Our staff is working feverishly to care for those admitted and to identify the cause of this unfortunate incident,' the University Hospital's Medical Director said. 'The Iowa City community should remain calm and confident. We have one of the top medical facilities in the country and are prepared for all contingencies. We will release more information as it becomes available.'

The exact number of those affected is yet unknown, but an anonymous hospital source puts the numbers in the hundreds. The Federal Center for Disease Control has been called in, but has not released a statement. The Johnson County Sheriff's office declined to comment except to say, 'This is an ongoing investigation.'"

Several paragraph's speculated about possible causes: a rare contagion, a pathogen or poison in U of I food system.

'The U of I Food Service did not return our calls. But an unnamed source called it 'an act of bio-terrorism. This is Iowa's 9/11.' A hospital worker asked, 'Who would do such a terrible thing?'"

"He carefully refolded the paper, put it on the floor beside his dirty black sweatshirt and savored the sweet taste of success.

CHAPTER THIRTY-FIVE:
Cathedral

Friday, September 28, 2001

"I drove Brenda to her death," Herb Lovejoy admitted to Kelly. "We were on the Freeway in heavy traffic and I killed my wife and daughter. I took my eyes off the road."

"Why?"

"We were on a family outing. We were listening to Whitney Houston belt out *I Will Always Love You* when Paul tapped me on the shoulder and pointed out a bright red Pontiac Firebird passing us on the left. "Dad, that's what we need, instead of this old pile of junk!" I agreed with him. I was having a bit of a midlife crisis and had even been imagining myself as twenty, single and free. I turned and fixated on the beautiful red blur. That's when the SUV broadsided us. It was pulling onto the interstate and I didn't see it."

"That makes you a killer?"

"I got them killed," he lamented. "It was my fault. It was the same as pulling a trigger. I can't get the memory out of my mind. Some days I can't stand looking in the mirror.

I robbed Paul of his mother and sister."

"I guess I was wrong," she sympathized. "You probably can understand my feelings. That sounds way worse than slugging a cop."

"It is!"

Kelly challenged him, "I'm going to get the best lawyer money can buy to fix my screw-up!! What are you going to do?"

"I don't know," he mumbled.

"You can't go on hating yourself."

"No."

"I thought you Christian-types believed in forgiveness?" she challenged.

"We do!" Something woke up inside Herb.

"But not in your case?"

Thumping his chest, he replied, "Forgiveness is supposed to be for everyone. I've preached that a hundred times! God forgives. God forgives anything."

"How do you know?" she asked. Herb paused a long time before answering.

"Jesus, loves me...this is all I know for sure," he said.

"Jesus supposedly died for us?"

"Yes." The prisoner led the preacher back to what he believed.

Herb said, "Jesus forgives us and wants us to forgive."

"Forgive ourselves?"

"Yes. Something I've obviously failed to do."

She said, "Sounds like we could use a double-dose of forgiveness!"

"We could!" The guilty preacher reached out and took her hand. "Forgiveness is there for both of us." The jail became a cathedral.

CHAPTER THIRTY-SIX:
Freedom

Friday, September 28, 2001

Their reflective moment was broken when an officer opened the door, "Miss Sanders, you've been cleared. Your prints weren't the ones found at the Kerr farm. Chief Curtis told me he's dropping the assault charges but expects you to do community service - maybe volunteer at the Johnson County Humane Society or something. You're getting off easy. Lucky for you, Phil Curtis is such a gracious guy. He makes me proud to be a Methodist Christian." Not pressing charges also saved Chief Curtis a ton of paperwork and an embarrassing trial. Few cops would want to admit they'd been decked by one blow from a 5'3" teenage girl.

"You are free to go." Kelly wanted to hug the deputy.

Lovejoy asked, "Officer, what's happening with the investigation?"

"You must be the only one in Eastern Iowa who doesn't know," the officer replied.

"Know what?" Herb asked

"That the Johnson County Police and The Iowa State Department of Criminal Investigation are hot on the killer's trail!"

"Killer?" Herb looked confused.

The deputy said, "Three students at University Hospitals died this afternoon."

"Must have happened after I left the hospital," Herb answered. "It was bedlam there! We didn't get much sleep last night."

"You were there?" the stunned deputy asked.

Herb pointed to his U of I chaplain's ID badge.

The deputy gulped and then apologized. "Chaplain, you've been in the middle of all of this. I'm so sorry."

Kelly interrupted, "Mr. Lovejoy, I want to go home. Can you please take me?"

"Be glad to. Your home is where my son is."

"And my Darth!" she said. The deputy handed Kelly a sack filled with her pre-arrest belongings. She gladly changed into her own clothes. She had her life back.

As they walked outside to Herb's car, the officer called out urgently. "Miss Sanders. We just got word that your mother and father are flying in from New York tonight."

"Thank God," she said.

CHAPTER THIRTY-SEVEN:
Unwanted

Saturday, September 29, 2001

"Mamma, you made me do it!" Ratman ranted. "Papa would have been proud. I engineered my own poison plane to take down academia's towers. I shut them down and got away with it." He giggled like a five-year-old, "No one will remember last week's stupid Hawkeye game but everyone will remember what I've done!"

But in the depths of his dark soul, Daniel Ratinsky wanted to forget. He wanted to forget his childhood. He had been a puny kid who was bullied by everyone. He endured demeaning nicknames like Runty Rat, Ratboy and Ratface. His 2nd grade classmates couldn't remember his last name, Ratinsky; what would they have done with his immigrant grandfather's name, Ratinskousky? Daniel played with bugs instead of classmates and enjoyed dissecting toads. He called it 'slicing and dicing.' He graduated to killing a neighbor's cat, gutting it and stripping the muscle from the bone. His mother caught him and beat him bloody before rubbing the cat's blood into his face. Ratinsky hated all women, especially her. Once in a drunken moment, she had hugged him, "Give me a kiss, my little Danny boy." That alcoholic slobber made him hate his first name, too.

Before his mother passed out, she'd blubber out popular love songs. Daniel hated love songs. They made him think of her.

But Daniel Ratinsky got smarter and his mother never caught him experimenting again. He kept killing. The neighbor's barking dog irritated him, so Danny explored ways to kill the rat terrier. The eleven-year-old decided to sprinkle rat poison in the dog's water bowl. He waited until the neighbor and his mother were at work. 'How much will it take?' He tried a teaspoon full. It took three days to shut up the nagging mutt. Danny's interest in science, chemistry and biology continued growing. 'What makes things live? How do they die?' Ratinsky studied venoms, carcinogens, mutagens and toxins. They sounded like even more fun than rat poison. When his mother was at work, he continued his dark experiments in his father's abandoned garage laboratory.

In school, he excelled in the sciences and spent every possible moment in chemistry and physics laboratories. He did gruesome experiments at home, but fooled his mother into thinking they were school assignments. Danny got a new nickname from his classmates- 'Lab Rat.' He called himself, 'Lab Rat Ratinsky. He aced his way through the hardest high school classes, but never lost his fascination with killing.

His sophomore English teacher asked him what his favorite story was. He told her, "Moby Dick." It was a lie he thought she wanted to hear, but Melville's classic was not his favorite story. Ratinsky preferred a simple story he'd found in a children's book. He liked it because he could twist the expected ending to fit his purposes. It was a morality story meant to teach youngsters to make good choices. But young Daniel read it another way.

"Once there was a clever, bright little boy who wanted to stump his teacher. The boy asked his teacher two questions, 'What do I have in my hands?' 'Is it alive or dead?' Feathers sprouted from the boy's fist and the teacher guessed, 'A baby bird?' The boy asked his second question, 'Is it alive or dead?'" Ratinsky knew how the tale was supposed to end. The teacher should say, 'The answer to the question and the bird's future is in your hands.' But Daniel Ratinsky gave the fable his own special ending, "The clever boy holds up his fist and squeezes the life from the bird. 'It dies no matter what you say. I can kill!'"

CHAPTER THIRTY-EIGHT:
Feds

Saturday, September 29, 2001

"**M**r. President, thank you for returning my call," Iowa Governor Tom Vilsak apologized. "We have a deadly situation and need your help...."

George W. Bush responded, "Governor, I've already been briefed about what happened in Iowa City. There is no room for partisan politics in a time like this. We have to work together."

"I agree sir," Vilsak responded. "We have a crisis out here. My Division of Criminal Investigation experts think it could be another terrorist act. Nothing official has been released to the media yet, but rumors are growing. I knew you'd want a heads-up on any hints of terrorism. I heard your speech to the nation."

He had the President's attention. Bush wanted to know a.s.a.p. about anything connected to 9/11. He had declared 'a war on terror' in his address to the Joint Session of Congress nine days earlier. He didn't want any surprises or distractions from his objective "...to defeat terrorism as a threat to our way of life...to stop it, eliminate it, and destroy it where it grows." Bush remembered the standing ovation Congress gave him for that line.

The President told Vilsak, "Iowa will get full access to all possible federal resources."

"Thank you, Mr. President. That's what we need."

A few minutes later, Bush's FBI Director Robert Mueller got the call. The President said, "I don't want to find terrorism growing in Iowa's corn fields. If it's there, I need to know immediately."

FBI Director Mueller, who had been on the job in DC for only three harrowing weeks, telephoned Chicago Special Agent Mike Kovalcik. When his phone rang, Kovalcik was loading his heaviest fishing tackle into his truck, eager to catch some Lake Michigan trout. He'd signed up for a half-day charter expedition out of Montrose Harbor. When he heard Director Mueller's voice, he knew he'd caught something bigger than any trout in Lake Michigan.

"Mike, this is Priority One from the Big Guy himself," Mueller told him. After briefing him on the Iowa crisis, the Director warned, "This could be a terrorist attack in the heartland trying to poison our food supply. I want you and your team in Iowa immediately."

Kovalcik hesitated before asking, "Isn't that Nebraska's jurisdiction?"

"Yes, but this is a special case," Mueller said. "I want this headed up by someone I know. I haven't forgotten your work in DC in '95."

"Thank you, sir. How will the Omaha Field Office fit in?"

"I'll smooth it over with them."

"I assume there are agents already in Iowa?" Kovalcik asked.

"Several," the Director responded. "The agents closest to Iowa City are based in Cedar Rapids and Davenport. I'll call Omaha. In a few minutes I'll get everyone on board. Mike, I want you to coordinate this. Put together an investigation team with Omaha, Iowa's D.C.I. and the locals. No turf wars, no infighting with state investigators or with the Omaha Field Office. We're soldiers in the same army and we're under attack. Any resources you need are yours. This is do or die trying! The President wants this resolved yesterday!"

Kovalcik didn't flinch, "Sir, I will tell you what we need. Fly our best DC techs out to Iowa. I think Cedar Rapids is the nearest airport. Put them on the plane yesterday."

Mueller didn't blink either. He knew how much hung in the balance. "You need to get this done Mike, or you'll be on a plane to your next appointment in Minot, North Dakota." That was the most remote, coldest place the director could think of.

When the director hung up, Kovalcik phoned his team. "Director Mueller has ordered us to Iowa, immediately. Bring your full gear and be in our parking lot in 90 minutes. We'll take our SUVs and our tech vans. Driving to Iowa will be as quick as getting in and out of O'Hare Airport and we'll have our own wheels and equipment. Who knows what they have out there? I'll brief you on the way."

The FBI caravan was a noisy black blur barreling west down I-80 toward Iowa. Sirens and flashing lights didn't bother Kovalcik. He updated his team as they traveled. "Three students are dead. We're looking for a killer. This is way beyond murder. Hundreds of innocent Americans have been hospitalized. Sound like terrorism to you?" He didn't wait for their answers. "Co-operate, pool resources with state and local cops, Iowa's DCI and CDC and the Omaha Field Office. No turf battles- that's an order straight from Director Mueller. This crisis is already hitting the networks. Stay focused. High productivity with low publicity is our goal. I don't want to waste time coddling camera crews or doing interviews. "We've got a job to do. Don't get sucked into the media blizzard."

Agent Maria Gomez was glad that Kovalcik's tracking skills were better than his allegories. She thought, 'Media blizzards don't suck you in. They blow you over and freeze your behind.' But she had worked with him long enough to know when to keep her mouth shut. Gomez had earned more than her share of promotions and knew some co-workers were jealous and felt she'd made the grade because she was Latino. She knew better.

They crossed the I-80 Bridge south of Le Claire, Iowa and reached Iowa City forty minutes later. Kovalcik's SUV led the way. He was riding shotgun but left the navigation to others. The driver used GPS to get them to the county sheriff's office. GPS led them south on Dubuque Street, west on Washington, then south on Capital. The computer nerd fiddled with his laptop. "Listen to this, boss. The Johnson County website says, 'The County Sheriff's office leads in-depth investigations that may require special training....'"

"I feel safer already." Agent Gomez said sarcastically.

Closing his laptop, the FBI nerd quipped, "Their special training probably includes directing traffic, filling out forms and arresting drunk cows."

Kovalcik scolded, "Don't underestimate them! We need to cooperate. The locals will know stuff we don't. Remember, they live here. Natives can usually out-track outsiders."

Gomez knew he was right.

The caravan pulled into the Johnson County Sheriff's office parking lot. A uniformed officer rushed out to greet them. Kovalcik had arranged a meeting with all the law-enforcement players - county sheriff's officers, local police, Iowa DCI and CDC, University of Iowa, University Hospital, Cedar Rapids and Davenport FBI agents. The room was charged with nervous energy when the Chicago FBI agents stormed in.

After quick handshakes and brief introductions, Kovalcik took charge, leaving no doubt that he was Special Agent-in-Charge. "We'll set up a temporary Command Center here. Sheriff, we need space, computers, meeting rooms and access to all the phone lines you have. We need your absolute cooperation with no interference. This directive comes from the President himself." He diagrammed the chain of command on a white board. Everyone in the room had a place on the roster. He'd brief the Omaha crew when they arrived.

The University Public Relations officer asked, "What about communication? Who'll control that?"

"The sheriff's communication director and our Chicago FBI specialist will handle public relations," Kovalcik said. "No interviews without pre-clearance and no leaks. Now people, let's get down to business. You have twenty minutes to fill us in on what happened. Who did this? Why? How do we get them?

"I'll start," a doctor from University Hospital said. "It's a mass poisoning affecting more than 400 victims, mostly students. Three students are dead, twenty are in critical condition and as many as fifty are paralyzed. Dozens more with horrific symptoms are being admitted, even as we speak. The numbers are going to get worse before they get better. We are still unclear about the most effective course of treatment."

"What's the cause?" Kovalcik asked.

The chief of Iowa's Department of Public Health answered, "Our tests indicate that it is a toxin. The University of Iowa Food Service dispensed contaminated milk to students on Wednesday and Thursday." The U of I public relations man winced; this was a PR nightmare.

"What do we know about the toxin?" Kovalcik probed.

"It's a bacteria called Clostridium Botulinum," said the chief.

"In English?"

The medical officer explained, "It's deadly in its purest forms. But the FDA has approved it for limited use and medical research. You'd recognize the name 'Botox'?"

"I do, but it's more of an LA beauty thing." The Chicago team smiled. "Later, doctor, you can help us understand how this toxin works. You remember the old cop adage, 'Trace the weapon; catch the killer.' Anyone know the source of the toxin?"

"A local dairy plant processed the milk," the Iowa DCI chief replied. "But we've pretty much cleared them as the point of origin. The milk was probably contaminated before it was delivered to the plant."

Kovalcik said, "Thanks, we'll double check that. My team will need to interview some of the victims. Are they connected in any way? Was this random or targeted violence? Do you have leads, theories, suspects?" Several ideas were floated in the group.

"Let's work the motive angle, Kovalcik said. "Obviously, we have to consider the possibility of another al Qaeda terrorist attack. Poisoned milk could kill a lot of people. Might be part of a terror network here in the Midwest. Has anyone claimed responsibility for this? A terrorist attack in the heartland would paralyze people. If Americans can't be safe here, we can't be safe anyplace."

The Cedar Rapids agent added, "Maybe the 9/11 attack was a catalyst or a trigger for some crazy guy?"

"Could have been a crazy girl," a female team member chided.

"We've already eliminated one female suspect," the Iowa DCI Director responded.

"Stay focused," Kovalcik scolded. "Who might be angry at the University of Iowa? Could be an unhappy student, a mad scientist, a crazy Botox doctor, a rival football team? Let's not rule out any options until we have solid leads."

Kovalcik assigned FBI Agents to work with state and local police in teams to address three questions: Who poisoned the milk? How? Why? "We're going to hit the ground running. Communication people, keep this zipped up until we get these terrorists. He updated headquarters in Washington before they left Iowa City Command Central.

CHAPTER THIRTY-NINE:
Anniversary

Saturday, September 29, 2001

Farmer Jerry Kerr and wife Marilyn needed a break from the milk poisoning nightmare. She took his hand as they walked to the shed where Jerry's fancy F-150 Ford pick-up was parked. He was proud to drive an American-made truck. He bought it new on 9/9/1999. Last year he'd asked her why they hadn't picked a wedding date that was as easy to remember. Using her teacher's voice, she had chided, "Mr. Kerr, sir, you will remember that we chose our wedding date to fit into your silage chopping and fall corn picking schedules. Saturday, September 29 was the only one that would fit your schedule." She smiled.

But, she didn't lecture him too long. They were celebrating their 35th wedding anniversary. Jerry held the truck door open for her, just like he did on their first date. He could be a gentleman if he tried. Jerry started his beloved truck and the country station kicked on with the engine. It was Kenny Chesney's familiar voice. Pulling out of the driveway, the lyrics of *All I Need to Know* were perfect for their anniversary,

"… Rain or shine, you'll be mine tonight.

That's all I need to know
In a world where most things come and go
I'll always have you to hold
And that's all I need to know..."

They were driving into West Branch when the song ended. She squeezed his arm, "Did you know that song was going to be on, just now?"

"Sure did. I asked Kenny to sing for us tonight. Timed it pretty well, didn't I?" he joked.

They were headed for a fancy Iowa City restaurant. He'd even made reservations, though Jerry preferred the more down-home cooking at The Cove, east of West Branch. It was known for home-made apple pies. He licked his lips at the thought of the hot fresh pie, with two scoops of vanilla ice cream. When they pulled onto I-80 and headed west toward Iowa City, Jerry's appetite switched gears. He began anticipating a delicious steak, well-done, not-bloody. They walked arm-in-arm into the Highlander restaurant. When they were seated, Jerry wondered why they didn't turn up the lights so folks could see to order. Marilyn enjoyed the calming effect of the candlelight. She thought Jerry looked so handsome in his tie, reminding her of their wedding day. The night spot was a little rich for his blood, but he owed it to her. Both enjoyed the food. Jerry kept trying to work up the courage to tell her the truth but decided to wait until the drive home. When he backed out of his parking spot they almost got hit by two black SUVs barreling into the lot. "Watch out, you maniacs!" he yelled, noting the Illinois license plates.

On the way home, Jerry began telling Marilyn his dark secret. She got the deer in the headlights look. The romantic mood vanished like a snuffed candle.

"What now? How do we fix this?" Marilyn asked as he opened the kitchen door. Jerry couldn't bring himself to look at as his wife of 35 years.

He flopped into his favorite chair, looking more like a whipped puppy than her bull-dog of a man. "I don't know how."

She sat on the arm of his chair and put her arm around his shoulder, "Jerry, you know how to fix anything."

"Not this." He couldn't look at her.

CHAPTER FORTY:
Obsession

Lab Rat Ratinsky knew about secrets. He had lived in dark, secret places his entire life. As a boy, he found refuge from his mother's brutality in his grandmother's normalcy. Gram Ratinsky doted over him; fed him cookies and usually let him have his way. She didn't shout at him or hit him. Being with her was peaceful, except for Sunday mornings and Wednesday nights. Her church scared him. It was the hell-fire and brimstone, the end-of-the-world, everyone-else-is-going-to-hell kind of church. They shrieked, shouted and screamed. It scared him because it felt too much like home.

Daniel sat with Gram on the 3rd row on the right side nearest the aisle. She liked to be close to the front so she wouldn't miss anything. Daniel occupied himself by counting the tiny panes of glass in the old stained glass windows. The building had been abandoned by a mainline church fleeing to the suburbs. A new church moved into the dilapidated gothic building and launched a ministry to save the world. Daniel soon learned the rhythm of the services- small talk, loud prayers, enthusiastic singing, long bible readings and thunderous preaching climaxed by a frantic altar call. People stumbled forward, weeping and wailing. Daniel was never one of them. Gram usually was.

The preacher's favorite bible texts were from the books of Revelation and Daniel. When a Daniel passage was read, Gram would nudge him, "That's who you were named after." The Book of Daniel had interesting stories – one described how God's prophet Daniel survived a night in a lion's den; another pictured three men walking alive out of a fiery furnace. But it was the wild Book of Revelation that truly captured his imagination.

No matter how hard he tried, Daniel could not banish the memory of one especially fiery sermon from Revelation. It filled him with fear and fascination. Fascination morphed into obsession. The ranting preacher's pictures of hell were too vivid. The words and images infested his mind: demons, monsters, punishment, rivers of blood, judgment and death.

"Hear the Word of the Lord. Hear it and fear it, O sinner. Listen and weep. Squirm and shout. Judgment is coming. Without the Lord God, you belong to the Beast." The preacher waved the open bible over his head, "Revelation 13:7-8. The hellish beast with the dreaded number 666 tattooed on his head. 666!" The boy was stunned when the preacher repeated the number. 'How could it be? No. It wasn't possible!' Daniel had twice counted the number of pieces in the big stained glass windows. Both times he got the same total - 666.

Daniel couldn't chase that dreaded number from his mind. The fierce beast with 666 tattooed on its head chased him through his nightmares every night. His wounded young mind fixated on that number. In high school, he dreaded seeing any number even close to the Beast's number. If a number sequence got beyond 646, he'd break into a sweat.

Once he vomited in an advanced math class. The teacher asked what was wrong but Daniel couldn't admit that the number 666 reached out from his computer screen and choked him. Another time, he missed getting a perfect test score because he couldn't bear to write down the correct answer 6-6-6. Daniel researched his obsession and found that professionals would diagnose him as having 'hexakosioihexekontahexaphobia', the debilitating fear of the number

666. The young scientist cured himself by writing the number 666 for two solid days. He filled four notebooks by hand then entered the grisly numbers into his computer. It took a ream of paper to print them. Daniel purged the dreaded number 666, but wasn't able to banish the beast within.

CHAPTER FORTY-ONE:
Investigation

Saturday, September 29, 2001

Special Agent Mike Kovalcik and his team deployed their plan, systematically following the poison's trail beginning with doctors and victims at the hospital; then to the two biggest university dorms, where they questioned the café staff. The tech team examined milk dispensers. Kovalcik's tracking procedures led them to the Dubuque Street Dairy on the edge of town. The state health director confirmed the initial conclusion that the toxin was already in the milk when it was delivered for processing. Agents sorted through test results and did some of their own testing. They found nothing to contradict the health department's assessment that the milk had been delivered from Kerr Dairy near West Branch, the primary source of fluid milk for the University's Food Service.

"That dairy farm will be our next stop," Kovalcik announced, "After we get some food and a short night of sleep. The farm isn't going anyplace." His exhausted team was relieved.

The Omaha agent who'd joined them mid-afternoon, said, "Glad to hear that. I'm starving!"

"There's a fancy restaurant connected to the motel we booked you into," the Johnson Country Sheriff suggested.

"Fancy is fine, if we don't have to pick up the tab," the frugal Omaha Agent said.

The team piled into their black vans and SUVs and followed the Sheriff's white cruiser. The caravan skidded into the restaurant parking lot and almost broadsided a Ford 150. "Careful, he's as big as we are."

Flashing FBI badges got them a separate meeting room. As they ate, Kovalcik asked, "Where are we?"

"Other than in the middle of a big cornfield?" quipped another Chicagoan.

"But remember," Kovalcik reprimanded, "Iowa corn fattened that juicy steak you're chowing down at taxpayer expense."

"OK, you got me there! But I will tell you what I think about the case. This farmer, Jerry Kerr, had access to the milk before it went to the processing plant. Farmers know about chemicals and stuff. He could have staged the flask thing before the trucker ever got there. Maybe he was angry at something. Kerr was a Vietnam vet, maybe he suffered from Post-Traumatic-Stress-Disorder. P.T.S.D. can make you do crazy things."

"Good hypothesis. We'll start with him bright and early tomorrow morning."

CHAPTER FORTY-TWO:
Full Disclosure

Saturday, September 29, 2001

Jerry Kerr faced down his personal beasts, "The war messed me up, Marilyn. When my buddies and I came home, no one knew about post-traumatic stress disorder. Whatever you call it, I had it. This milk terrorist scare brought it all back. '65 was a dark place. I named it my 'Foxhole from Hell'." She started to speak, but he stopped her, "I have to say this! I was in that dark place before I met you. You were light and I crawled out of my Hell Hole to be with you. But when we lost the baby, I crawled back in." She understood his pain about their baby.

"That's where I've stayed." He pushed her arm away, stood up, reached behind the cushion and yanked out a whiskey bottle. Jerry threw it across the room. "That's one of my secrets!" Both watched the bottle spin across the floor into the doorway.

She put her hand back on his shoulder, "Jerry, I know you drink some. But you said you really don't like it."

"I don't! But it helps dull the darkness. This is my fault!"

"What is? What do you mean?" She asked.

"Spin the bottle, wherever it points is my fault. What's the point? When we lost the baby, I knew it hurt you, but I couldn't talk about it. I have dark secrets," he cried.

"Jerry...."

"No. I'm finally talking about it. Let me finish." He unloaded a truck-load of memories. "I should have kept the milk house locked. I didn't have enough security. I should have seen it coming. We could lose everything...." His voice trailed off into despair.

"We won't!" She said and hugged him. "But there's no room for two of us down in your damnable dark foxhole." He shrugged and grunted. "Jerry, you are bigger than this. You can beat this. Life is too precious to give up on it. You have a big heart. You get teary-eyed when a cow dies. You don't have to retreat into that foxhole." He saw that she understood; she knew there was something he hadn't told her yet. She continued, "Remember Christmas Eve when the pastor said the darkness could not put out the light? Then we each lit a little candle and those candles pushed the darkness away. Christ is the light. Maybe it's time to crawl out of the darkness toward the light?"

He pondered her words. He was raised a church kid, Sunday School and the whole nine yards. He had joined the West Branch Methodist Church when he was 13, but his faith development stopped there. In contrast, Marilyn had not been a church girl, but she was changed at a summer church camp near Fairfield. It turned her on to the Lord and transformed her life. She went to the University of Iowa and got involved in the student Wesley Foundation. Her faith got sharpened by conversations there. Methodists again! His stern Methodist grandfather's advice hobbled into his mind, "Jerry Franklin Kerr, don't do anything in the dark you don't want seen in the light of day."

Jerry sobbed, "I'm tired of the darkness. I'm as scared as I was in that firefight in Plie Me. I'm scared by what I became that day."

"Became what?" Marilyn asked.

"A killer!" he said, jabbing his finger into his chest.

She said, "Jerry, that was war. You were trained to kill the enemy."

"Marilyn, I've been too ashamed to tell you this. I didn't kill just the enemy. I killed one of my own. We were caught in a cross fire and I heard something behind me. I turned and a figure lunged toward me through the elephant grass. I fired five rounds. The impact spun him around and I saw his face and his uniform. He was bleeding red, white and blue. We had marched together into that killing field and I had killed him. He was dead. I crawled away through the grass like a snake. I never even told my best buddy Mike."

"Oh honey, what a terrible secret!" She slid into his lap and wept with him. At last the painful truth was exposed. When their tears dried, Marilyn put her hand under his chin and forced him look at her. "There are two big differences between you back then and you now: you've figured out how bad the darkness is and we can go together toward the light. And you know today that I will always love you."

"Sweetheart," he said, "I love you too and I promise no more dark secrets, I need more light. I need you to help me find it. I need to go to church with you tomorrow."

CHAPTER FORTY-THREE:
Breakthrough

Sunday, September 30, 2001

Police Chief Phil Curtis sat at his kitchen table enjoying a second cup of coffee with the Sunday paper when the feds barged in. He cinched his bathrobe as they flashed their badges and demanded that he accompany them to the Kerr Dairy Farm. Curtis got dressed quickly, then led the FBI caravan through the rolling Iowa country side. They pulled off the blacktop road onto the gravel. City drivers, not used to gravel roads, skidded into Jerry Kerr's driveway just as he finished milking. Special Agent Kovalcik walked to the barn and confronted Kerr and all but accused him of being a terrorist.

Jerry was incensed, "Why would I poison my own milk? What kind of idiot do you think I am? I could lose everything. I was told you guys had prints from the flask. That should have cleared me. I'm a veteran and I'm already in your data base."

"We'll double check that, Mr. Kerr. Do you know your service number?" Kovalcik said.

"Not off the top of my head. My official service card might be buried back in Nam for all I know. But you can look me up. How many Jerry Franklin Kerr's from West Branch, Iowa served in Nam in 1965?"

"I'd guess not many. We'll have to confirm your story. You have a phone we could use?"

"In my office," Jerry pointed, "through that door."

It took ten minutes for the FBI's Sunday computer gurus to find Kerr's prints. They called back, "Corporal Jerry Franklin Kerr's prints do not match the ones on the broken flask."

"Isn't that a shock?" Jerry sneered. "I dumped my milk down the drain to keep the public safe. I sure as hell didn't dump poison in it."

"Sorry, Mr. Kerr, we're just following protocol and eliminating suspects," Kovalcik's quick apology reflected his deep respect for veterans.

"You can take me off your s-list," Jerry said. "If you gentlemen will excuse me, I promised my wife I'd go to church with her today." Kerr shouted over his shoulder, "Hope you find some real suspects to harass."

Kovalcik stood in the driveway and popped his knuckles in frustration, not wanting to admit they had nothing; no motives, no leads. But he had to stay positive and be both quarterback and cheerleader. So he addressed his team, "Dead ends and restarts are like dandelions in spring grass."

They drove back to Iowa City. When they walked into the command center, the DCI announced, "Sir, we caught a break!"

Kovalcik, Gomez and the team gathered around the DCI's computer. "What do you have?" their leader asked.

"The bio techs from DC fine-tuned the identity of the toxin. It's identical to the type the University of Iowa is using for medical research and treatments."

"I didn't think we'd find it at Wal-Mart!" Kovalcik exploded. "Where does this lead us?"

"Like you said, sir, 'track the weapon and find the killer'.

Kovalcik asked impatiently, "Where did the toxin trail begin?"

"The University of Iowa's Bio Med Research Center," the computer tech said. "We've contacted the University and the department head will meet you there."

"Where is this Bio Med Lab?" Kovalcik asked.

"I'll show you," Iowa City's Police Chief said. "Back in the day, I was assigned the University Hospital beat."

"No sirens, but full-speed!" Kovalcik ordered.

CHAPTER FORTY-FOUR:
Evidence and Suspects

Sunday, September 30, 2001

The jangling phone ended Ruth Sander's Sunday afternoon nap. She fumbled to answer it and got a gruff order from her boss. "Dr. Sanders, you need to go to the Bio Med building immediately!"

She tried to shake the cobwebs out of her head. "What's the problem, sir?"

"The FBI traced the toxin used in the milk poisoning to your lab," the Medical Director said.

"They what?" she blurted.

Her heart sank as the director continued, "The Botulinum which poisoned the students is the same strain you're using at the lab. Federal Agents are on the way to the Bio Building. I need you go meet with them. Consider the liability we may face. We want justice done but we don't want the University to become another victim!"

No one needed to decode the message for her. She pulled on a suit jacket, grabbed her purse and rushed to her car, forgetting to even leave a note to her family. Sander's heart was pounding to the rhythm of 9/11. Driving south on Highway 1, she pondered. Who? Why? How? Biological sciences were easier to figure out than human nature. Sanders parked in her reserved spot in the back of the building and sprinted toward the front door. A small army of very serious men and women waited for her there.

A square jawed agent, about her age, said, "We're in a big hurry to catch a terrorist or terrorists. I'm Special Agent Michael Kovalcik, FBI. This is my team."

"I'm Dr. Ruth Sanders. I direct this lab and its research…."

The agent interrupted, "Why don't we go inside and talk?" It wasn't a question.

The PHD fumbled to unlock the front door. Others usually did it for her. She led them into the lobby. Her agile mind raced, searching for clues about how an act of terrorism could come out of this building and her lab. She had dedicated her life and research to helping people.

Kovalcik and his team followed her. The lobby had the stale smell of a weekend office, laced with chemicals he didn't recognize. His team circled Dr. Sanders as he said, "Let's cut to the chase, the toxin has been traced to your laboratory. Everyone with access to your lab is a suspect until we clear them…including you."

She choked on the irony. Like her daughter, Kelly, she was now a suspect. "I can narrow your suspect pool. Very few people have access to the Botulinum in this lab. It's kept in a secure refrigerated storage facility."

"How many have access?" the woman agent asked.

"Three," Sanders replied.

"Who are they? We need their names!" Agent Gomez demanded.

"You don't have to use that tone with me," Sanders responded. "I'm not hiding anything. Only three of us had access to the toxin. I knew the code. So did the lab supervisor and a doctoral student."

Gomez replied smugly, "So you are one of three possible suspects?"

"There are really only two," the researcher corrected. "The lab supervisor is in Germany at a research seminar."

"You and the doctoral student?" Kovalcik asked.

"Yes."

"Who is this student?"

"Daniel Ratinsky," she replied.

"Why did he have access?" questioned the female agent.

Dr. Sanders explained, "Ratinsky led a research group studying Botulinum as a treatment for Parkinson's disease."

Kovalcik was impressed. "I had an uncle who had that. Parkinson's is bad stuff! He didn't get to do any fishing when he retired; he was confined to a wheel chair for years. They find a cure?"

"Regrettably not," she replied. "In fact, the research project is being terminated because of funding problems and lack of progress."

"When did this happen?" the Omaha agent asked.

Sanders said, "I notified the grad students about two weeks ago."

"How did they take the cancellation?"

Dr. Sanders replayed the meeting in her mind. "They responded as you'd expect: surprise, resignation, disappointment, anger."

"Who showed the most anger?"

"Ratinsky, the doctoral student, had invested the most and had the most to lose...." Sanders realized what she was suggesting. It was unthinkable that someone from the University community would do this terrible thing.

Kovalcik watched Sanders closely. His gut told him she was innocent, so he focused his attention on the doctoral student, "How many students worked with Ratinsky?"

"There are four others in the group."

"Could they all have been involved?" the Omaha agent probed.

Sanders hesitated. "I'm new here. I really don't know them that well; but I don't recall much camaraderie in the group. The others usually went along with Ratinsky; he had seniority."

"Was he angry enough to be violent?" Kovalcik asked.

"I don't know. But he was upset enough to phone me at home to complain," she said.

"Could you pull up his records?" Gomez asked.

Sanders knew about student confidentiality, but the gravity of the situation and the stares of the agents, led her to cooperate, "I usually let others search our student databases...."

"Humor us," Gomez chided. She hated top brass who felt they were above routine tasks.

"Agent, I'm not stonewalling," Sanders explained. "I'm just not familiar with the computers in this room."

Sensing the growing conflict between the women, Kovalcik asked politely, "Dr. Sanders, would you please go to your office and look him up on your computer? While you are checking, please access information on the other four researchers as well. Then you can take us to your not-so-secure toxin storage facility."

Ten minutes later, Sanders handed them a stack of bios and photos of the students and led them to Lab #2, where the Parkinson's research was done. She pointed to a locked refrigerated safe behind a rack of test tubes, "That's it!"

"Open it!" Gomez ordered.

"...If you please," Kovalcik interjected. Agent Gomez finally got the message.

Sanders took two pieces of paper out of a folder. One had the entry code numbers for the safe. She handed the other sheet, a printout, to Kovalcik. "This is the toxin inventory list. Federal Law requires us to update it monthly."

Kovalcik looked at the list, "It's dated September 1, 2001. OK, open the door, doctor." Sanders complied.

The racks of vials and tubes meant nothing to the agents until Sanders exclaimed, "It's gone!" She was so shaken that she had trouble pulling on her rubber gloves. She picked up a vial, then another and held them up to the light. "Empty." They searched the room for evidence, boxed papers and impounded computers. Kovalcik made a formal request to take evidence from the room.

Sanders said, "The University Hospital Medical Research Department will give you whatever we have that might lead to a solution."

"Our solution is to make an arrest that leads to a conviction," Kovalcik said. "Until we make an arrest, Dr. Sanders, this must be held in absolute secrecy. You will be in violation of federal statues if you even tell a family member about our investigation. Until this is resolved, do not leave town." Sanders nodded, regretting that she'd rushed to Iowa City without calling her husband first. Kovalcik turned to his team, "Dr. Sanders has provided us with bios and photos of all five members of the research team. Two of you will investigate each of them." Copies were passed around. "But our primary suspect is Daniel Ratinsky. Run him by our profile team. Find out all you can about him. Agent Gomez, I want you and a local to stake out the suspect's residence. Be careful not to spook him. We'll have an assault unit on standby. Call us when you have eyes on the perp."

Special Agent Kovalcik called FBI Director Mueller and reported their discovery of the empty toxin vials and the primary suspect. "Director, we're getting close. Unless he's fled the city, we'll have him soon." Mueller asked about possible 9/11 connections.

"Sir, we think it's a lone terrorist; no evidence yet of any links to 9/11."

Shortly after sunset, Gomez called Kovalcik, "We got him. We've got him! Ratinsky just walked into his house. The lights are on. I can see him. Send in that swat team."

CHAPTER FORTY-FIVE:

Capture and Interrogation

Sunday, September 30. 2001

Daniel Ratinsky didn't see them coming. Police in riot gear stormed his house, with guns raised. "We have a warrant for your arrest!" They mirandized him, cuffed him roughly and pushed him toward the police car. No TV cameras recorded the arrest; the communication lid was still tight.

An officer smiled when the perp bumped his head on the squad car door frame. The driver glared back through the screen, "You've ruined a lot of lives. I hope you are miserable back there!" Ratinsky was temporarily bewildered. When they got to the county jail, the cop taunted him, "Want something to drink? How about some milk we saved from a campus lunch room?"

Special Agent Mike Kovalcik watched through the one-way window as suspect Daniel Ratinsky was marched into the interrogation room and pushed into the chair facing the window. The cameras were running. The Federal Magistrate would soon join the officers in the observation room and had authorized them to begin the interrogation. The goal was a confession and a conviction. Agent Kovalcik, the DA, a DCI investigator, the prosecuting attorney, the Iowa City Police Chief, Johnson County Sheriff and the Chicago FBI's best computer geek crowded into an adjoining room to plot their interrogation strategy.

Agent Gomez joined them and asked, "What's the plan? Good cop, bad cop?"

"We'll get there eventually," Kovalcik replied. "Let's soften him up first."

The District Attorney said, "Kill him with kindness! We can outsmart this schmuck!"

"We just got new background information on the perp. Daniel Ratinisky is brilliant academically. He is crazy smart," The Special Agent said.

Gomez said, "Crazy, that's for sure!"

"What else do we know?" the DA asked.

"He grew up in a single parent family in L.A."

The DA said, "We already knew that."

"We've been in touch with LA's finest and they're checking out his college years."

Kovalcik turned to the computer pro and said, "See what you can uncover on family, friends or neighbors."

Gomez asked, "How long do we keep him waiting?"

"Let him sweat!" her boss said. "Get the arresting officer out of there and give the perp some alone-time. We'll study him from here."

The DA asked, "Special Agent Kovalcik, are you any good at reading body language?"

"Top dog!" Kovalcik replied. "For instance, your body tells me you've had too much to eat, too little exercise and maybe too much to drink." The DA pretended to be offended, but he'd been nailed. The arresting officer joined them. They asked him, "What role do you want in this interrogation drama?"

"I'm already the bad cop. He figured that out in the squad car ride over here."

"OK, then stay in character," Kovalcik said. "You be the bad cop and I'll start out as the good cop. What's your impression of the perp from the arrest?"

"We surprised the hell out of him when we busted him, but he seemed to recover pretty quickly. I think he thinks we can't get him for this."

"Let's surprise him again," Kovalcik challenged. When the three of us go into that room, I want the rest of you to watch and listen. Hang on to every word. Look for weaknesses we can exploit later. Better fill your java cups; it's going to be a long night. Gomez, you take the perimeter, the arresting officer and I will take the chairs. This is cat and mouse. He's the rat and we're the cats."

The DA said, "Hope he doesn't lawyer up."

Kovalcik warned his team, "Don't show your hand too early. Let me lead." The watchers saw the trio enter the room. They heard the suspect breathing and the chairs scraping.

"Mr. Ratinsky, I'm Agent Kovalcik. Are you still cuffed? Officer, take those cuffs off, show this man a little respect." The officer unlocked the cuffs and Ratinsky rubbed his wrists in relief. Leaning toward the suspect, Kovalcik asked, "You need anything - coke or coffee? The coke is standard stuff from a machine. I wouldn't brag about our cop coffee." Ratinsky hesitated.

"Go ahead. What'll it be?"

"Coffee, black," the prisoner replied. He needed his caffeine to stay alert and guard against cop tricks, but he knew he was much smarter than they were.

"Gomez, get this man a fresh cup of Joe," Kovalcik ordered. She left the room, unsuccessfully trying to hide her irritation. The DA behind the glass watched the perp's eyes follow Gomez out of the room. Something was off and didn't feel right.

The arresting officer got in Ratinsky's face, "Hope you get a crappy cup of coffee, you piece of...."

"Take it easy, officer." Kovalcik interrupted. "We're here trying to get to know each other and to clear this up. Mr. Ratinsky, tell me about UCLA. I hear it's a top-notch school. Not many can get in, let alone graduate. You're part of a pretty exclusive club!"

Ratinsky broke his vow of silence and bragged about his undergraduate achievements – double major in biology and chemistry, graduated with highest honors. "In fact, I was class Salutatorian."

"That must have made your mama proud," Kovalcik said casually.

Ratinsky stiffened.

Kovalcik, sensing he'd struck a nerve, backed off, "UCLA with honors is a great start. How did you get to the University of Iowa? I hope I got that right. We out-of-staters always confuse the University of Iowa and Iowa State University."

Flattered, the suspect boasted about his Master's Degree and his doctoral program in Bio-Med at U of I. "My compliments for keeping the two Iowa Universities straight."

"You a researcher?" the agent asked.

"Yes."

"Did I read that you are trying to cure Parkinson's disease?"

"Our research is promising," Ratinsky boasted.

Kovalcik knew this was a pivotal point. He pretended to be impressed, "Your innovative research used the Clostridium Botrinoluemis bacteria?" He intentionally mispronounced the toxin's name.

The suspect corrected him, "Actually the name is Botulinum. Botox is made from it."

"Really?" the agent said. "How much do you know about this bacteria?"

"Pretty much everything! Nobody knows more. I'd say I'm the best. The best there is," he smiled at his cleverness.

"Is that what you used to kill and injure hundreds of Iowa students?" Kovalcik accused. Ratinsky exploded out of his chair, bumped the table spilling his coffee and knocking two file folders to the floor. The interrogator got exactly the reaction he wanted.

Gomez leaped in, "Officers, restrain him!" She jerked him back into his chair.

Twisting as they re-cuffed him, Ratinsky screamed, "You don't know anything Mr. Agent man. You were just jerking me around, fishing with your empty hook. You won't trick me!"

Special Agent Kovalcik put the folders back on the table and leaned in to the suspect, "Your mama must be proud to have nursed a cowardly baby terrorist who kills college kids with poisoned milk. What do you have to say now, Punk!"

Ratinsky spat in his face. Kovalcik didn't flinch, but bellowed, "We'll talk again, you airhead scumbag. You can drink your next cup of coffee in Hell!"

The trio returned to the Observation Room and Kovalcik asked, "What did you think?"

One observer said, "You didn't make a new best friend."

"You got nothing," complained the DA.

"Too kind," the angry Iowa City Police Chief said.

Special Agent Kovalcik shrugged, "We're just getting started. We'll let him simmer, stew in his own juices. Anything we can use to pry him open?"

"I found an interesting thing," their computer guru said. "It may not be significant, but seemed outside the norm...."

"Tell us!"

The agent at the keyboard said, "Ratinsky was on UCLA's honors list, but his parent's names weren't published."

"How is that important?" Kovalcik asked.

"Sir, all the other students had parents' names and home towns listed; but he didn't."

Gomez said, "That is odd."

"He had a strange reaction when you mentioned his mama," the DA said. "And he had a weird way of looking at Gomez."

She agreed, "I think the DA's on to something. The perp shut down when you talked about his mother. He's hiding something."

"We'll have to find that special something!" Kovalcik exclaimed.

The DA jumped in, "We might have a shot. This guy hasn't lawyered up yet. We can keep peeling away the onion."

"I'd rather cook the onion," the arresting officer said.

"We can turn up the heat," the DA responded. "As long as he thinks he's smarter than we are, we can get him."

"We just got something, boss," the computer guy reported. "LA was able to interview some neighbors where he grew up. Several said his mother is a lush. Two officers went to the house and talked with her. She was sober enough to talk, but juiced enough to let us into some of the family closets."

"What did they learn?" Gomez asked.

"When the officers told her that her son was being charged, she wasn't surprised. Mama Ratinsky hasn't spoken with her bright-boy son in years."

"Or they talked last week and she's forgotten already," Gomez said.

Agent Kovalcik asked, "Anything else?"

"It may be nothing," the tech answered, "but a next door neighbor said, 'That crazy kid hated animals. When he was ten, he skinned a cat in the back yard. When his ma caught him, she beat him. The whole family is nuts.' The LA officer said neighbors seemed eager to tell this stuff. No love lost between the neighbors and this family."

"Might just be a neighborhood feud or it might be the key that unlocks the puzzle," Kovalcik said. Gomez wanted to correct him and say keys unlock locks, not puzzles. But she held her tongue.

"Sir," the tech guy interrupted," there's more here on the interview with Rat's mom. She told the officers she knew something like this was going to happen. 'I tried, but I couldn't handle him. It's my fault, my fault!' It sounded like drunk-talk, until she described Danny's father...."

"Ratinsky's father? Do you have the LA cop's phone number?" Kovalcik asked.

"I do sir. Do you want me to call him?"

"Hook me up now."

Kovalcik jotted down notes as he got the whole story again from the LA officer. It was always better to hear first-hand. He was jolted when the LA detective said, "Sir, the mother told us that her husband abandoned them by committing suicide. 'The coward left me to raise his crazy bastard boy by myself!' Those were her exact words."

"That's it," Kovalcik shouted. We have the ammunition to bring down this terrorist. The crazy genius's childhood animal killing sprees have metastasized into mass human killing. He is mad as hell at his mother and is still trying to earn his dead father's approval."

The DA said, "Mike, you've got him. Chum the water, throw out the bait and hook this monster."

Kovalcik said, "I only wish I could have hooked him a week ago. Let's reel him in."

CHAPTER FORTY-SIX:
Setting the Hook

Sunday, September 30, 2001

The trio stepped back into The Box, known to civilians as The Interview Room. "Daniel Ratinsky, we have bad news for you," Kovalcik said. The suspect stared at the table, clenching his fists and straining against the handcuffs. "We're ready to charge you with terrorism and multiple counts of murder. 9/11 has sharpened our legal knives and we've got hard-edged evidence. All you can do now is to help yourself by telling us the truth."

Kovalcik leaned in, "Want to see it? Look at it!" He shoved a sheet of paper into Ratinsky's face. "It's the memo authorizing you access to the secure vault where the bacteria is stored. You had the combination. See it here in black and white, second paragraph, first line. Your friend Dr. Ruth Sanders found this for us."

"She's not my friend! You're framing me. Someone stole my code…." The watchers saw Ratinsky twitch at Dr. Sander's name. They'd struck another nerve.

"That excuse isn't worthy of your IQ. But you've been making excuses for yourself your whole life." Ratinsky glared. Kovalcik pressed, "Not only can we prove you did it. We know why."

"You just think you do. What do you know? You stupid cop!" The suspect countered.

"You're the stupid one. Your research grant was cancelled and you struck back at the University the way the terrorists struck New York City...." Ratinsky tried to twist away from his interrogator. "But you've needed to do this since you were a sick little boy."

"What do you mean?" Ratinsky demanded.

"You needed to earn your father's approval, show him you're smarter than everyone else," pressed Kovalcik.

Gomez chimed in, "But you failed didn't you. You failed your dad. That's why he offed himself." Ratinsky came unglued, screaming obscenities until his voice got hoarse. The investigators waited him out. They'd heard all the words before.

"Was killing your dad just a warm-up for the college kids?" Kovalcik asked.

"I didn't kill my father. He killed himself!" screamed Ratinsky.

"Did you hear that Gomez? Killing runs in the family," chided Kovalcik.

She replied, "Must be genetic."

"Genetic mutation of the worst kind," Kovalcik said. "Morons mutating into monsters."

"My father wasn't a moron! He was brilliant," screeched Ratinsky.

"But you are a monster, Ratman," Kovalcik prodded. "I bet you thought about killing your mother, didn't you?" Ratinsky squirmed. The Box was heating up. Kovalcik chummed the water with the monster's family blood, waiting for the right moment to set the hook.

Gomez said, "The wimp can't face it. He hates all of us women, especially moms."

"But you didn't have the guts to kill her, did you?" Kovalcik challenged. "You slimy little coward! You killed innocent kids. Why didn't you keep the killing in your family, where it belonged?"

"I never had a family! My mother hated me and my father abandoned me." He began to cry.

"So, you poisoned the milk to hurt them?" demanded Kovalcik.

"No! No! That's not why I did it. I don't need to kill my mother; she's been dead to me for years. She's killing herself with her booze! Father killed himself."

"Why did you do it then?" Kovalcik, sensing the kill, set the hook.

"I did it for revenge! I couldn't let them get away with it. They deserved to be punished and I figured out how to do it."

"So you admit poisoning the milk?"

"I did it. What do you want, a signed confession?" Bingo. The big fish hit the bait.

"That would help. We also want to hear your side of the story. Dr. Ruth Sanders wasn't sure you had the smarts to do it." Kovalcik played the suspect the way he'd play a fish on his line. "You're the only one who really knows what happened. We're just dumb cops. Why don't you tell us how you did it?" Ratinsky was relieved. He had no one to talk to and was about to explode from the built-up ego pressure. The cops saw a strange calm wash over him. "Go ahead. Take your time." Kovalcik's voice softened, "We'll even give you another hot cup of coffee." They poured it and Daniel-Lab-Rat-Ratinsky poured out his story.

CHAPTER FORTY-SEVEN:
Evil Deed

Monday, October 1, 2001

"I was in the diner watching 9/11 reruns and mulling over what Dr. 'Slash' Sanders and the idiots at the University had done to me. 'They have to pay! They have to pay! They have to pay!' Revenge became my mantra as I watched the planes repeatedly taking down The Twin Towers. I thought about how the jet fuel in those planes turned them into deadly weapons. I knew I needed a deadly weapon to use on Sanders and the University. That's when I was inspired." He sipped some coffee.

"What inspired you," Kovalcik asked.

"A glass of milk."

Gomez asked, "ONE glass of milk led you to do this?"

"What would you know, you stupid cow? You weren't there. I ordered milk. When I drank it, I remembered an article I'd read in *JAMA, The Journal of American Medical Association*. When I tell you the title, even you will understand why it was a 'high and holy' moment." He imitated his Gram's Pentecostal preacher's voice. They waited. "The article warned, 'Botulinum Toxin…a Biological Weapon.' Get it? A biological weapon. It was written by renowned civil bio-defense scientists." Gomez's skeptical frown prompted him to say more, "If you don't believe me, you can read it yourself. The February 28, 2001 issue told how a single gram of toxin could kill thousands. Genius's like me remember stuff like that."

"What did it have to do with milk?" asked Gomez.

"The report warned that America's food supply was at risk for food borne botulinum poisoning. Our milk supply system was identified as a potential target. Milk became a perfect host for my perfect weapon – Botulinum! I know more about that toxin than anyone in the country, maybe anyone in the world. I knew how I could strike back." He paused, watching for their responses. "Dr. Sanders helped me to learn how to do it." They were confused. "Sanders forced my research group to do some silly public relations gigs: a cereal factory, a turkey processing plant and a dairy farm. We suffered through the big farmer's little lessons about milk production and shipping. But I paid attention. That hick farmer never knew he was giving me the guidance system for my weapon. I'd call it divine inspiration if I believed in that God hogwash. What are the odds - a random medical article, a glass of milk and a forced dairy tour? It worked together. It was genius. I did it, with a germ of help from the scientists, the waitress and the farmer." The Rat-Man sounded pleased with himself, proud of his evil deed.

"Sick," Gomez whispered to Kovalcik.

"I named my weapon 'Toxin 666.' That's the number of the horrible beast in the bible's Book of Revelation. Sorry, I'm sounding like Gramma's preacher. But I'm not afraid of that number anymore. It has a poetic demonic lilt – 666... 666... 666... 666...I got my revenge. I made them sick-sick-sick. 666 is my lucky number!"

"Your number is up Ratinsky," Kovalcik said. "And it wasn't a lucky number. You didn't get away with it. You will pay!"

"I already got away with a murder," the suspect bragged.

"What murder? Who are you talking about?" the officer asked.

"Dr. Smarter-than-Everyone-Engstrom," Ratinsky snorted.

TERROR IN THE HEARTLAND

The sheriff asked, "You mean the U of I prof who died at the Union?"

"That's the one. John Engstrom. I poisoned him too. You cops still don't know much."

"We know enough to put you away!" Agent-in-Charge Michael Kovalcik slammed his fist on the table. The terrorists in NY, DC and PA didn't get away with it and neither will you. Daniel Ratinsky, on behalf of the United States Government, I charge you with treason and acts of terrorism." The watchers applauded.

Johnson County's Sheriff stepped into the Box and intoned, "... Daniel Ratinsky, I charge you with multiple counts of capital murder, including Dr. John Engstrom."

Kovalcik telephoned FBI Director Mueller, "We got him. We got his confession and the whole nine yards! It was a single lone-wolf, nut-job killer, no connection to al-Qaida. Our techs will send the interview video to you. You will enjoy watching it. The President might like to see it, too."

Officers escorted Ratinsky back to his cell, his self-confidence deflated. He felt empty, utterly alone. His mother had locked him in the closet again. His inner void began filling with fear and dread as dark as that closet. 'No one understands. No one will help me!' He flopped down on the jail bunk and wept. He rolled over and knocked a handful of personal papers onto the floor. Ratinsky picked them up and absently-mindedly sorted through them. He found the hospital calling card sandwiched between his California driver's license and his yellow university parking pass. He twisted the card in his fingers, staring at the University of Iowa's gold dome logo, thinking about dead students and his dead life.

CHAPTER FORTY-EIGHT:
Resolution

Monday, October 1, 2001

Kelly Sanders propped her elbows on the Lovejoy's kitchen table. She, Paul and his father were waiting for the pizza to heat up. Herb had splurged on the best double cheese pizza at West Branch's Food-n-Gas Mart. Exhausted by the stressful week, they ignored the droning TV. Kelly reached down and patted Darth. She had brought her dog along to meet Mr. Lovejoy. Thanks to the jail crisis, Darth was now Paul's good-bud.

"How's the pizza coming, Dad?" Paul asked. Before Herb could reply, the evening news intruded, "Topping our news tonight, there has been an arrest in the Iowa City milk poisoning crime." Paul pumped his fist in the air, "Yes. Yes!" Kelly cheered and Darth barked. Herb was transfixed, his hand on the microwave. The Cedar Rapid's TV anchor described the intensive DCI and FBI search. "The accused was taken into federal custody and arrested. His name has not been released...."

They digested the news while nibbling on hot pizza. Paul burned his tongue with his first bite. The news restored Kelly's appetite. Nothing had tasted good since 9/11. Paul enjoyed watching the sparkle return to her eyes. She smiled impishly when Paul caught her sneaking pizza to Darth, who nuzzled her right leg.

For a few heart-wrenching days, Iowa had been in the national spotlight. The attack on the University of Iowa tore open the fresh wounds of 9/11. Network and cable commentators tried to name the Iowa disaster: "Milk-Gate" "Tank-Attack" "Toxin-in-the-Tank" "Dairy Disaster" "Terror-in-the-Heartland." No names stuck. The nation would soon forget what happened in Iowa, but Paul knew he wouldn't. Neither would Kelly. Herb left them at the kitchen table watching TV. When 'Wheel of Fortune' came on, Kelly asked, "Do you rural rubes really watch this old game show stuff?"

Paul winked at Kelly and pointed to Vanna White, "Sorry, I just like older blondes."

Kelly stood, struck a pose and hurried to turn off the TV. Before her hand touched the dial, Vanna's word magic disappeared and the channel 9 news anchor flashed back on the screen, "We have breaking news. Federal and state authorities have released the name of the milk terrorist, a Daniel Ratinsky."

Paul shouted, "Dad, get back in here! You have to see this."

The anchor continued, "The FBI and DCI report that Ratinsky, a disgruntled bio-medical doctoral student at the University of Iowa, was the sole terrorist. The Iowa City Police Department has released this mug shot." A blurred black and white image flickered on the screen. Herb thought the face looked familiar. Kelly agreed, but questioned, "Does anybody look like their mug shot?"

Paul teased, "You didn't like yours?"

She threw a pizza crust at him. He returned the favor.

Herb said, "Whatever you two mess up, you clean up."

The TV news anchor promised, "As authorities release more information, we will interrupt our regular broadcast with the story." The teens cleared away the pizza remains and wiped off the plastic picnic table cloth that covered the table. Ruth Sanders phoned and asked Kelly if she'd seen the news. Both mother and daughter were relieved to no longer be suspects. Herb put the milk jug back in the fridge and heard the State DCI Chief being interviewed about the milk terrorist. "What will be next for him?" the reporter asked.

The officer ticked down the list of state and federal charges and what kind of sentencing the terrorist would face. Not realizing he was still on camera, he blurted, "The SOB deserves to die. Even death is too good for him!"

That candid comment did not surprise Herb, but his own response did. Instead of churning hatred toward this evil-doer, he felt a strange surge of sympathy, empathy or something more. 'That's odd?' he thought. Herb's insight crystallized with a fresh connection to Jesus' extraordinary words about loving enemies and praying for persecutors. He walked into the living room and picked up his bible. It fell open to the Gospel of Matthew. He was stunned by the familiar words. He read them again and again. Herb telephoned Connie Baughman to tell her what he'd discovered.

Paul and Kelly sat in the kitchen, oblivious to what was going on in the adjoining room. Paul absently stroked her hair, while she stroked Darth. Her dog half climbed into Kelly's lap and licked her face. She gladly accepted the kiss and realized Paul was watching. "Don't be jealous, I have enough kisses for both of you."

Paul leaned over and kissed her just as his dad walked in with his open bible.

"Hey, listen to this!" Paul thought his dad sounded ready to preach. He was. "I just read Jesus' words in Matthew 5:43-44, "You have heard that it was said, 'You shall love your neighbor and hate your enemy.' But I say to you, 'Love your enemies and pray for those who persecute you.'" Do you see how that connects with the tonight's news and the 9/11 terrorists?" They shrugged and looked at each other. "Think about it! Who are our enemies? Who caused you to be persecuted, Kelly?"

"Mr. Sicko terrorist Bio Boy!"

Herb responded, "That guy is our enemy but he's also the guy Jesus wants us to love."

"You're kidding!" they said.

"I've never been more serious. I'm forty-five years old and finally get it. I spent fifteen years preaching and I missed the real message. We need to love the enemy who is right here in front of us. We need to love the one who has hurt us most - the nastiest, meanest, most despicable person we know. We're to love the one who is so filled with hatred that he does unthinkable things. American justice will swallow him whole. Rightful anger from all over Iowa and across the nation will rain down on him. He will be absolutely abandoned. He is our enemy. I have to reach out to him, God help me." They stared at him.

"Dad, what are you going to do?" Paul asked in disbelief.

"Jesus said to pray for those who persecute us. I can do that, right now. Tomorrow I'm going to find out where he's jailed and visit him," Herb promised.

CHAPTER FORTY-NINE:
Jail Visit

Tuesday, October 2, 2001

The next morning, Herb climbed the steps to the Johnson County Jail in Iowa City. He was so focused on what he was doing that he didn't notice that he was whistling, 'I will always love you.' He was determined to do what Jesus wanted him to do. But, armed guards, not Jesus, welcomed him in the lobby. "Empty your pockets into the tray and walk through the metal detector." Many feared that what happened in Iowa was an extension of the 9/11attacks. Two stern men with ear pieces and black suits questioned him. They had Fed written all over them. The pair escorted him into the cramped jail waiting room and pointed to the counter topped with glass to the ceiling. The receptionist asked tersely, "Who you here to see?"

When Herb said, "Daniel Ratinsky," the officer glared at him and nodded to the agents. They stepped closer, almost breathing down his neck.

"So you're here to visit the damned terrorist?" the deputy asked.

"Yes, I am. And even that wretched terrorist has a name."

"Sure he does. I'd call him 'Damned Crazy', even if his mother named him Daniel Ratinsky. You're his first visitor and that's one more than he deserves; but regulations force me to do this." He scrolled through the list. "Here he is. I'll see if he's preapproved you. What's your name other than Enemy Lover?

"My name is Herbert Lovejoy. I don't mind being called an enemy lover."

The clerk cracked up, "Lovejoy. Lovejoy." He laughed until tears rolled down to his blue collar. "Lovejoy! I don't believe it. But if that's your real name, I guess you always travel with love and joy together. Love gives you joy!" He laughed so hard he almost slid off his desk chair. "OK, joker, show me your ID." Herb pushed his chaplain's card through the mouse hole in the glass. "I guess the jokes on me, Reverend Fool. I'll page upstairs and see if the perp will see you". He flicked the intercom switch, "Hey, Bobby, some do-gooder is here to see the king of the scumbags. Will you see if his Lowness will grant a visitor? OK. Get back to me right away. I'm sure Reverend Loves-Everybody has an army of terrorists to cuddle up to before the sun sets." He pointed to the four-chair waiting room, "Have a seat. I'll tell you if King Ratman grants you an audience."

Ten minutes later, the policeman beckoned Lovejoy back and recited the usual how-to-visit-an-inmate spiel. The dull recitation reminded Herb of a flight attendant's safety speech. "Slide your driver's license through the slot. Go through the door behind you and you'll find an intercom button. Tell him who you are...." He chuckled again, "But Bobby may not believe you either. So identify yourself and the prisoner you want to love until he finds some joy...." More laughter erupted. The mocking of his last name was nothing new. Herb had heard it since grade school.

Herb stepped through the doorway and the heavy metal door slammed behind him. He walked across the hall, identified himself and pushed the elevator button. Lovejoy stepped off the elevator and was escorted to a folding chair facing a wall of safety glass. He waited, watching the empty chair on the other side of the glass wall. When the inmate, wearing handcuffs, was escorted in, Herb wondered, 'Do I know him?' Their eyes met.

Herb picked up the phone. But before he could say anything, Ratinsky raised his arms and held out a scrap of paper. Herb's nose almost touched the glass as he leaned forward to see what it was. Then he knew. It was his University of Iowa Hospital Chaplain's calling card. He remembered the campus diner.

Herb breathed a prayer, "Lord, what do I say?"

CPSIA information can be obtained
at www.ICGtesting.com
Printed in the USA
FSOW02n0511181116
27489FS